The Abbot's Dilemma

A Sherborne Medieval Mystery, featuring Matthias Barton

By

Rosie Lear

Grosvenor House
Publishing Limited

This book is published by
Grosvenor House Publishing Ltd
Link House
140 The Broadway, Tolworth, Surrey, KT6 7HT.
www.grosvenorhousepublishing.co.uk

This book is a work of fiction with some reference to
actual historical events and persons. The story is
the product of the author's imagination.

A CIP record for this book
is available from the British Library

ISBN 978-1-83975-820-1

Remembering Angela
August 2021

Acknowledgements

Bob & Mil Chimley for proof reading and technical help.
Cover: an original illustration by Neil Pockett

"Civil dissension is a viperous worm
That gnaws the bowels of the commonwealth"
Henry VI...William Shakespeare.

Heavy type indicates historical figures of the time.

Characters of Sherborne.

Abbot Bradford, Abbot of Sherborne Abbey, an arrogant Abbot

His prior, William, a softer version

Thomas Copeland, schoolmaster of the Abbey school, wise and just

Dame Maud, housekeeper at his school, sensible and homely

Dame Margaret Goffe, a wealthy widow of Sherborne, upright and generous

Mistress Amice, a local seamstress, a very private person

Arnet, her adopted son, lively and innocent

Dionisia, a common gossip of the town with nasty ideas

Amelisia, a gentle herb seller, trying her best

Daniel and Noah Jolif, troublemakers certainly not doing their best

John Woke, a mysterious stranger

Edmund, the bishop's reeve

Tomas, his son

Townspeople, assorted...Glovers, Hoddinottes, Vowells

Characters of Milborne Port

Matthias Barton, schoolmaster and occasional sleuth for the Coroner

Mistress Alice, his wife, daughter of the coroner and an able teacher

Luke de Bhun, her son, step son to Matthias

Davy, Matthias' man servant, faithful and hardworking

Elizabeth, his wife, a darn good cook

Rose and Betony, young daughters of Matthias and Alice, both poppets

Lindy, their nursemaid, competent

Silas, friend to Luke, a bit spoiled

Martin Cooper, friend to the family, crippled by the wars in France

Lydia, his wife and helpmeet, a sweet girl

Freya, Lydia's daughter

Ennis, their adopted daughter, a clever lass

Finn, a pupil of Matthias, trouble ahead.

Various assorted villagers

Other characters of importance

Bishop Ayscough, bishop of Salisbury, never where he should be

Ezekiel Jacobson, friend of Matthias and gifted barber surgeon

Sir Tobias Delaware, Coroner of Dorset, an upright man.

CHAPTER ONE

A beginning

Thomas Copeland gazed from his window at the setting sun behind Sherborne Abbey. He was disturbed by the increasingly unruly behaviour of the good people of Sherborne, which seemed to be spreading even to his pupils. There had been small acts of civil disobedience throughout the town increasing as the days passed, and he was afraid that these excited his scholars, some of whom were eager to be involved, seeing it as daring and bold.

Now into his sixtieth year, Thomas wondered whether he was becoming too old, maybe even intolerant of such behaviours. His scholars had tumbled out of the schoolroom in high excitement today, anxious to be part of a street procession, but Thomas was afraid it was turning into a riot of dissatisfaction rather than an orderly procession. They should, he felt, be celebrating the arrival in England of Margaret of Anjou, the young King's wife, soon to be his crowned queen, but the main celebration of that was of course in London, far from Sherborne, so not the thing uppermost in their minds.

Luke de Bhun had chosen not to accompany his fellow students, remaining in the hall of their lodging house. At twelve years old, Luke was a gentle, serious youth, more thoughtful and wiser than many of his fellow students. His stepfather, Matthias Barton had high hopes for the boy, believing him to be a suitable candidate eventually for the halls of Oxford or Cambridge.

"Are you not outside with friends, Luke?" Thomas asked him kindly.

Luke smiled politely at his stepfather's mentor and old teacher.

"They will find trouble today, Sir. I am wondering how my grandfather is faring in London. He was summoned to attend the celebrations together with representatives from other shires. I hope he has some good stories to tell us when he returns."

Luke's grandfather, Sir Tobias Delaware, was the King's coroner for Dorset but also a justice of the peace, and had travelled up to London with a small retinue to witness the coronation in the capital of the young queen, just fifteen years old. Luke was keenly interested in the affairs of the young King Henry, followed his actions as far as he was able and applauded the foundation of the college he had founded in Eton, near to Windsor. His step father, whom Luke much admired and loved, was a school teacher himself, even admitting one or two girls into his small school in Milborne Port.

"He will have some good stories to tell, Luke, when he returns. I look forward to you being able to pass the details onto us in the schoolroom when you have heard his stories."

Luke thrilled at the idea that he might be able to re-create the processions, the cheers, the pageantry of the occasion to his fellow students, although he knew some would not enjoy them. Already there were those among the general populace as well as students, who were divided in opinion about the young king who was so unlike his well-loved father, the fifth Henry. The sixth Henry was gentle, philosophical, country loving, peaceful and, unfortunately, not much liked for his inability to take decisions. The country as a whole were delighted that he had taken a wife, believing that the dynasty of the nation would now be assured when Henry did his duty by them and produced a male heir.

A commotion outside in the street grew nearer, louder and more insistent. The door burst open and a gaggle of young students burst in, panting, excited and full of bombast.

"Luke, you missed the fun...but it didn't end well....the bailiff was called...I think the man was injured...he was bleeding....he shouldn't have argued with the players..."

"The players?" Luke interrupted, "was Merrik with them?"

Merrik, one of the chief players, was a friend of Luke's family and Luke enjoyed watching Merrik's players perform on their great travelling cart.

"I don't know – we didn't get close enough...they were organizing their cart for a show..."

The excitement and telling of the fracas continued round and round for a little while until Dame Maud appeared to quieten them and instil some order into their chaos. Luke listened as they described the sudden overflowing of disagreement into fist fights, turning ugly when a wicked looking dagger was pulled and a thrust to the body stilled the crowd.

"Who was it?" Luke asked, looking from one to the other of his fellow scholars. Their flushed, sweaty faces and quickened breath told of their heightened enjoyment at the sights they had seen. Luke didn't like it. He had once been at the mercy of knives, aggression and fear and had no wish to return to that scenario. It had taken him a long time to recover from that experience which had marked him in ways he did not wish to recall.

"Henry Goffe had the knife..." Titus told him. "The bailiff was called....I don't know who the other man was. Henry Goffe has a terrible temper on him. I hope the man isn't dead. if he is, it will be the worse for Henry."

Dame Maud shepherded the boys into their dormitory, but the excited chatter continued as she tried to calm their noise. Luke became withdrawn from the noise, - it was his exit strategy from situations which took him back to the frightening times of six years ago. He fastened his thoughts on the calm of his home, his mother, his two young half sisters, now two and four, and Matthias, the guiding light for Luke of his whole life.

The bailiff knocked on the door just as she was beginning to calm the hubbub and asked to speak to the boys who may have seen the affray. Several boys hustled to be the first to speak, but he was firm with them, only wanting those who had actually been close enough to really see clearly what happened.

"We need your Grandfather home to deal with some of these hotheads, young Luke," he said, as he rejected several scholars who were obviously just wanting to join in the "fun". Luke agreed wholeheartedly as the bailiff left.

Sir Tobias, from his mounted position towards the rear of the vast crowd, watched the advancing procession. The aldermen and merchants of the city were all dressed in the colours chosen by the leading aldermen of the city, hand stitched. The brilliant blue of their garments echoed the dazzling blue sky on this May morning, and their red hoods were embroidered with the crest of the profession of the wearer, making a sea of colour. The city was ablaze with noise, cheering crowds, people expectant with hope for the future. Both England and France had endured several years of poor harvest bringing poverty but this appeared to be in the past now, and hope flared for the future, a peaceful time with the suggestion of an heir for the King. Margaret of Anjou would surely provide a fertile breeding ground.

Sir Tobias patted the neck of his powerful destrier, restless in this crowd. He thought on the unfolding events of the past few years, both political as well as personal. King Henry had exhibited a leaning towards education and good works. He had founded a college at Eton, sponsored a place of higher education in Cambridge especially meant for the poorer clerks of the realm, indeed, closer to home, he had licenced the alms-house of Sherborne, much worked upon by the good citizens of Sherborne and surrounding parishes. Of warfare, however, there was no leadership. He was not the same man as his father. Decision taking had not proved his metier, and thus Humphrey Duke of Gloucester, and Cardinal Beaufort together with My lord Suffolk had provided a confused and often conflicting series of policies over which the troublesome lords in government had often squabbled.

Gloucester's wife Eleanor had provided a scandal in court circles which led to his own downfall; she had predicted the death of the King, even giving a date for this event, 1441, which led to her being damned as a witch and sentenced to enforced imprisonment. Her divorce from Gloucester was inevitable and she was at present incarcerated in a remote Kent castle, Gloucester himself being as side lined as Cardinal Beaufort, who had made serious blunders abroad, losing the English their final chance to win back some land in France. With these two statesmen thus side lined, Suffolk was now the leading light, with Richard Duke of York snapping at his heels.

Suffolk had travelled to France in 1444 to attempt an end to the disastrous warfare, and returned with the hand of fifteen- year- old Margaret of Anjou as a bride for Henry. As was the custom, Suffolk had stood proxy for Henry and in front of huge crowds in Tours Cathedral had slipped the wedding band onto Margaret's finger to cheers from the gathered nobles. Now, a year later, Margaret was here in person.

Sir Tobias reflected on her arrival, as told to him by the Sheriff of Dorset, the last time he had been in Dorchester. The Sheriff had been summoned to Southampton as Sheriff of a neighbouring county to witness the arrival, in April just past, of Margaret. She had arrived by sea, an unpleasant journey made worse by her sea-sickness. The Sheriff recounted how thin and pale she was, looking like a sickly girl without the strength to disembark without considerable help. However, she had travelled to Titchfield Abbey, where Henry met her and in the quiet solitude of the Abbey, married her in person.

Would she look better now, he wondered, glancing round at his fellow knights, all summoned to witness her arrival in London to be crowned. It reminded him of how shocked he had been when his grandson Luke had returned home after the abduction he had suffered. Luke had been thin, pale, full of nightmares, clinging to Matthias, who had rescued him from the smugglers. It had taken several months before the nightly terrors ceased, but on the birth of the Coroner's first granddaughter, Luke had turned a corner and although still a quiet, serious boy, never looked back. He was thankful for his son-in-law's steadying hand on the family and for his quick brain and willing help in some of the more puzzling incidents locally, albeit in a private capacity, assisting him willingly in the important work of justice.

What changes he had seen over the last few years, he mused, squinting against the sun to see into the distance as he heard cheering from afar. The procession had started...it was coming from The Tower, where Margaret of Anjou had been lodged for the last two days. He hoped she would look improved. It wouldn't do to look sickly on this feast, which was to last three days.

Sir Tobias stood up in his stirrups to see better. There – she was coming into view now – clothed in brilliant white garments and carried in a litter the better for all to see her. Behind her and moving with her were the blue and red aldermen of the city. Cheering crowds greeted her, flags and pennants fluttered in the light breeze – what a stupendous day, Sir Tobias thought. What a great beginning for a new start for the young King.

The city was looking as good as it could, - huge efforts had been made to clean every thoroughfare, every gutter, every piece of brickwork. The wooden steeple of St. Paul's had been struck by lightning during the Winter, but the city excelled at making a feast day to be remembered. Player's carts abounded on every street corner, with pageantry denoting the purity and grace of the new queen, Margaret of Anjou. As Sir Tobias turned his horse towards home with his fellow travellers three days later, he would remember, somewhat wryly, this celebration of hope in the years to come.

Matthias invited Sir Tobias into the schoolroom some days later to talk to the scholars about the celebrations he had witnessed. It was important, he believed, that the young should understand what was happening in their world, and who better to tell it than Sir Tobias, who had been present. Matthias' scholars ranged in age from seven years to eleven. He now had increased his space, using a barn outside as a schoolroom for the younger boys, where Alice, his wife and the daughter of Sir Tobias, taught them. Matthias himself taught the older boys who had, over the last few years, been joined by two girls. Some of his earlier scholars had graduated to the school in Sherborne, run by Thomas Copeland, among them, Luke and his friend Titus. Matthias was hopeful that one or two who had passed through his hands might go on to study in the schools of Oxford or Cambridge.

As Sir Tobias painted a vivid picture for the scholars of the great pageant which followed the coronation, Matthias studied his boys, noticing their re-action, wondering how many of them were truly understanding that this could be the start of a new era of prosperity for Henry and his young queen, - or not, if Henry continued to rely too heavily on the court advisors, all giving conflicting advice and building their own power base. Sadly, one or two scholars were influenced by their older siblings' opinions and they were restless at the mention of the young king, scepticism written on their faces. How could this happen to boys as young as eleven....ready to enter some kind of working life or continue their incomplete education? Had Luke been present he would have been enthralled by his grandsire's words but Matthias was troubled by the divisions that were appearing, even in his young scholars, and in particular, one lad Finn, son of Felstead, the miller.

Finn was older than the others, thought to be well turned twelve summers, and had joined the school in the previous year. He had needed some initial help from Alice to understand the basics of reading, and although he had shown an aptitude for learning, his writing skills were still shaky. However, he learned by rote fast and although was not an unpleasant boy, he had exhibited some very forthright opinions regarding the young king. Matthias had to remind him on several occasions that such opinions were best kept to himself lest he be accused of treachery. Finn had tried hard to comply, but Matthias noted that as the Coroner described the colour, the riches, the sumptuous food, the dancing, music, court masques and much more, Finn was becoming more and more sullen, lips twisted in a sneer. His normally pale complexion heightened in colour, his eyes were half closed and his fists were balled tightly. It was with a certain relief that Matthias watched him disappear with the other scholars into the yard for a break when Sir Tobias had finished, and Finn had controlled what Matthias feared would be an outburst. Matthias determined to speak with Finn later.

After his talk to the scholars had finished, Matthias and Sir Tobias sat together in the herb garden while the scholars jostled and played together. Finn was the centre of a small cluster of the older boys, and was giving vent to his feelings, but not so loudly as to be overheard.

"I am increasingly unhappy about the unrest in Sherborne," Sir Tobias told Matthias. "There was a stabbing whilst I was away – fortunately the young man was not seriously injured, but there are some hot heads in town who are causing some serious problems. The Abbot, as usual, is not helping matters along. There is talk about more disobedience around the issue of the font in the Abbey."

Matthias frowned, watching the younger scholars as they teased one of the boys. The two girls sat on the wall, watching; he had noticed that the girls were always denied the chance to participate in the rough and tumble, even if they wanted to, but he did not regret adding the girls. Ennis had been his first girl pupil, added in his absence some years ago by Alice. She was now too old for his school. She had done well, and was now helping her surrogate father, Martin Cooper, with his business.

"The townspeople haven't really moved on since the font in All Hallows was smashed years ago. The alms-house is now complete and has given much satisfaction to all, but the issue of the font and the rebuilding of the Abbey is still a matter that causes much friction in Sherborne."

Privately Matthias worried about Luke – was he likely to be involved? He knew the scholars were enthusiastic participants in affray….most young scholars were, - but Luke had seen enough trouble already in his young life to want to avoid any confrontation. He hoped Luke had enough sense to avoid becoming involved. At the mention of hotheads, Matthias glanced again at Finn, enjoying being the centre of the little group around him. Surely Finn was too young to involve himself….was there unrest in the village? Why had the miller decided so late to use Matthias' school for his son?

The hotheads mentioned by Sir Tobias were mostly young married men who remembered the fire in the Abbey - who could forget it? They were all Sherborne men, part of the very fabric of the town. Eight years on and the stained stones still told their story, as did the seemingly everlasting work of the rebuilding. It was slow, and the recompense demanded by Abbot Bradford caused much resentment. The Vowells, the Hoddinottes, the Cokers…..all families who gathered in some form or other to mumble and mutter and agitate against the Abbot, the monks, the Bishop of Salisbury. Between them, the Abbot and the

Bishop owned a great deal of property in Sherborne; rents were high, conditions sometimes harsh in the slender years of poor harvest and the changing face of the countryside had reduced the availability of labour. The Bishop's men had pulled out age old hedges to open up the countryside for the Bishop's sheep flocks. The Abbot, too, owned wealthy flocks which yielded a healthy income. The townspeople didn't see eye to eye with their ecclesiastical masters, but could this resentment have spread its tentacles out to the villages surrounding Sherborne?

Matthias and Alice sat long over their evening repast; The Coroner had left, Bettony and Rose were settled in their shared cot; it was a time for quiet contentment. Matthias loved this time, the ability to watch Alice's face as she sat opposite him; her clear blue eyes had kept their sparkle, her skin was still blessed with a youthful bloom. She had given him such a wealth of pleasure, two daughters whom he loved beyond anything, and her presence in any room lit his normal reticence into a spark. He wished his parents and late sisters could know how he had reshaped his life. He felt they would be proud of his achievements, but he knew he could not have achieved such calm without Alice's love. She, for her part, regarded Matthias with enormous love and respect. He had restored her son and her life to her after the terrifying abduction of Luke, at a time when she doubted she would ever recover from life's unfairness. She had grown in maturity, able to recognize that the strength of her love for Luke and her daughters was different from the love between husband and wife. There were still sometimes sparks between them, but these days they were easily resolved with humour.

They spoke now of the boy Finn.

"Is Finn ready to be with you all the time yet, my love?" Alice asked, leaning her elbows on the table, replete after the delicate stew Elizabeth had prepared.

Matthias swirled the wine remaining in his goblet as he considered. Was Finn ready? Would he like to see more of Finn with his group of boys?

"I suppose it would be good for him, but he has very strong leanings towards the troubled happenings at this time. His views are distinctly verging on rebellion."

"Are you afraid he will infect the others with his views?"

"Oh, that is already causing much animated talk....I noticed his reaction to your father's talk this morning. He cannot see that we need to give his Grace the King a chance to grow into his role. His marriage should prove a blessing."

"You would rather I kept him back with the younger boys for a little longer?"

"Has he mastered his letters adequately, Alice?"

She pondered carefully, remembering his dark head bent over the slate, carefully forming his letters and making sense of the words.

"Yes, he is a hard worker. Strange that he came to us so late."

"The family have had much trouble with older boys who caused dissent and unpleasantness in the home. Once they had left, the miller was able to look to Finn for his chances. I don't know the details, but when Miller Felstead approached me he gave an outline of their circumstances."

Alice yawned, stretched, reached her hands over the table to stroke Matthias' hands. He responded to her touch, rose and they gathered their empty dishes together. As he carried them out to the kitchen, he dropped a kiss onto her head, disturbing her wimple. She pushed her hair back as it escaped and followed Matthias to their bed chamber. Finn would be hers no longer. She was not sorry, - it said much for his desire to be able to read and write that he had been happy to sit some of each day with the younger scholars.

The weaver John Coker and his friends took to the fields surrounding Sherborne. It was a still July night, a rising moon hanging low in the sky. They had rough cloaks concealing their knives, hooded cowls pulled up over their heads. There was a sense of excitement and urgency about them as they skirted the castle and made for the meadows beyond, where one of the Bishop's great flocks was cropping the Summer pasture, lambs growing big enough to sell, adult sheep recently sheared by itinerant shearers, working fast for the Bishop. The wool would fetch a good price in the low countries although not as much as in the years previously, when English wool commanded a high premium, for now some of it was being used at home for weaving English cloth, a relatively new commodity. John Coker knew all about the price the Bishop would ask for his wool. A greedy man, the Bishop.

They sidled quietly over the damp grass, sliding now on their bellies. The gentle sound of grazing sheep, the muted crunch as the grass was pulled by individual animals, the rhythmic noise of jaws chewing the sweet Summer grass, the soft snorts of pleasure as the scent of the pulled grass was exhaled.....all these heightened the senses, gave them purpose, their intended disturbance to a peaceful, contented flock.

One man stood up carefully, moving stealthily, and with a rush of movement, threw himself bodily onto the back of a fat ewe, using his strength and his cloak to throw it expertly onto its back on the sweet grass. It struggled in panic, sharp, thin legs kicking wildly and scratching bare skin. Others bleated in fear and trotted away, causing a stampede in that part of the pasture. The man worked fast, slitting the throat first before beginning his butchering. They all joined in, their sharp knives knowing just where to go, warm blood on their hands enhancing the feeling of entitlement, staining their clothes. Breathing heavily, they dragged the sheep to the edge of the pasture near to the track where they boldly left the half-butchered carcass for all to see. The trail of blood from the butchering soaked the ground. With a collective grunt of satisfaction, the men shouldered their freshly butchered meat and prepared to go. Their first act of disobedience had been a success. It would not be their last.

CHAPTER TWO

This little piggy....

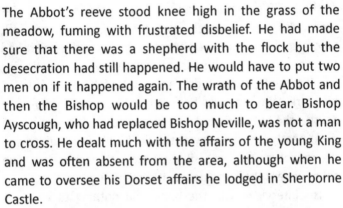

The Abbot's reeve stood knee high in the grass of the meadow, fuming with frustrated disbelief. He had made sure that there was a shepherd with the flock but the desecration had still happened. He would have to put two men on if it happened again. The wrath of the Abbot and then the Bishop would be too much to bear. Bishop Ayscough, who had replaced Bishop Neville, was not a man to cross. He dealt much with the affairs of the young King and was often absent from the area, although when he came to oversee his Dorset affairs he lodged in Sherborne Castle.

The reeve, Edmund, slung the remains of the butchered sheep over his shoulder and trudged down- hill towards the farm. Young hotheads from the town, he mused, determined to cause trouble, anxious to make their mark on the Abbey and add to the discontent in the town. He knew it wasn't just this town, - there had been rumours of civil unrest from neighbouring towns and beyond, brought in by travelling chapmen, tinkers, itinerant workers. Sherborne had additional troubles of its own, thanks to the ever-continuing argument about the smashed font and the payment due to Abbot Bradford towards the rebuilding of the Abbey after the fire.

Edmund grunted an acknowledgment as he passed two field workers resting by the track side. They looked askance at the carcass slung over his shoulder but made no comment. They were too aware of his power to dock them hours for lingering too long. Edmund was a conscientious reeve, making it his business to understand the circumstances of the workers on his lord's land. He had no desire to alienate workers without due cause. The slaughter of the ewe would have to be reported to the bailiff and the carcass disposed of. He sighed as he entered the gatehouse of the bailiff's domain. He would be questioned about his men, who was on watch, where had the ewe been left, whom could he trust. He shrugged; he knew the bailiff had to give account to the bishop eventually, so questioning was inevitable, but he didn't enjoy it. He felt he had failed in his work. Whoever was behind this knew what they were doing – the butchering had been well done - the best bits of meat neatly cut away. It was the deliberate insult of leaving the ragged carcass so visible by the track announcing the act of violent theft and desecration that angered him.

His interview with the bailiff did nothing to ease his mind. Although it was the first time such an event had occurred, there had been other acts of vandalism and destruction on the Bishop's land recently. His brief from the bailiff was simple; stop these happenings; search out the culprits; set better watches on the properties. Such things were not easy to achieve, especially as he had some strong suspicions concerning the culprits. He had his ear to the ground when enjoying his ale in the evenings, and was aware of clusters of young men chattering, whispering behind hands, gathering together in threatening groups on the streets always one step ahead of the watchmen. Nothing that he could put a name to, but the feeling of unease was there, and as a Sherborne man himself he was not entirely unsympathetic to the cause.

The Coroner had the same feeling of unease as he surveyed his list of cases a few days later. There were petty disobediences to deal with but far more than usual. Agitation towards the Abbot was increasing since he had acquired lands locally in his usual wily way...lands acquired through mortmain, a practice forbidden allowing the church to hold land belonging to the King with no taxes to pay. Abbot Bradford had acquired these valuable holdings worth £10 a year...a welcome addition to his building fund. The problem for the towns-people was that the Abbot required them to raise the money to pay for his licence to hold these lands; hard pressed as they were, the town had no choice but to dig deeper into their purse for the wily Abbot. Sir Tobias felt in his bones that this latest development was the root cause of the current increase of unrest and petty disobedience.

His list included the usual miscreants and offences – leaving stinking skins in the road – Sherborne was a big glove making town and the hides used left unwholesome residue behind – allowing tracks to become overgrown with brambles and thorn bushes, brawling in the streets, more common these days, and allowing pigs to wander the thoroughfares un-ringed. He paused over the two miscreants brought before him for street brawling – unkempt, insolent in manner, reeking of the midden. He remembered the name – Jolif –

"Sons of Robert Jolif?"

The two young men regarded him with a wary look of a sudden. They were identical twins, some twenty Summers each.

"So?" the bolder of the two spat, a sneer curling his lips.

"Mind your manners or you'll spend some time in the Castle prison."

The youth stood up straighter, looked the Coroner in the eye but did not remonstrate further.

"Don't make the mistakes of your father, young man. As I recall he was hanged for his persistent crimes. You boys would have been very young – babes. There's more to life than street brawling; What work do you do?"

"We labour for the Abbot." A surly answer, unwillingly given.

"Ah. "

The Coroner understood the implication. They would be given the worst tasks, and then only when there was work – it would not be regular, and the earnings would be meagre.

He dismissed the pair, fining them fourpence between them and watched them slouch out into the street. He had not been the Coroner when Robert Jolif, an outlaw, had been hanged, but he knew of him; he and his associate, John Seman had caused terror and mayhem in the surrounding area, Robert finally causing the death of an entire family by firing a cottage on the edge of the Bishop's deer park. He claimed it was a mistake, - he did not know it was occupied – he thought it was deserted, but his pleas went disregarded and he was hanged much to the delight of the populace around. He would advise the local bailiff and his watchmen to keep a beady eye on these two. He sensed trouble.

The twins winked knowingly at each other as they sauntered out into the crowded street. The Coroner had nothing on them – and he knew it. They re-joined their fellows in the Gooseberry Alehouse, smirking with a false sense of pride.

"The old fart can't touch us. What's a bit of fighting to him?"

There was no labour for the Abbot for them today – his reeve had stood several of them off being dissatisfied with their work. He had called their work little more than shirk and dismissed them. Now the twins had little coin, having been fined by the Coroner. They sat on barrels outside the Gooseberry, their black heads bent together as they planned their next irritation to the town. They had become nothing more than bully boys and rifflers, cut purses and braggers; true, their father had been a wolfshead, hanged for his crimes when the twins were mere babes, but the stain lingered on in them; they were resentful of any discipline, any attempt to curb their mischief. Some of the mischief was unpleasant, some of it was harmless but recently they had watched as their elders and betters had taunted the Abbot and Bishop, stirring up civil unrest in pockets in and around the town, and now emulated their behaviour, childishly but causing great irritation generally. Their mother had long gone, poverty and disgrace following her after her man was hanged. She had tried to return to her family in one of the surrounding villages, but they themselves had trodden the ladder of betterment, and had little time for the broken woman she had become. They had tried hard with her twins after she died, but the boys became unkempt, spiteful to their own children and wild.... when the boys ran off as they became older, they ceased searching for them and continued with their lives.

Daniel and Noah now moved off, having no further coin for ale, and left their cohort of friends behind them. They were making for Dionisia's place – a back street hovel on the edge of the town. Dionisia knew how to stir trouble, - she excelled in it, indeed, had been doing it all her life. She had appeared before the Coroner and the bailiff many times, been fined, spent time in the stocks, had been dunked unceremoniously in the river as a scold, -nothing cured her nose for trouble. She revelled in it. The twins loved her for it and encouraged her, learning new tricks for themselves but always a little more astute than Dionisia, so caught less often.

They found her squatting outside her squalid single storeyed hovel; dilapidated, dirty and smoky as it was, the young men found it appealing and squatted down beside her, anxious to discover what mischief Dionisia planned next.

Dionisia was of indeterminate age; scrawny neck, narrow mean face with button black eyes boring into the young men squatting in front of her, thin compressed lips over a few yellowing teeth, and a throaty chuckle as she listened to their account of their brush with the Coroner. She was a listener at other people's doors and windows, a grabber of opportunities, a woman with no soul, no morals, no kith and little kin. Her wispy hair hung round her face in greasy, tangled strands, and the two men watched fascinated as her claw like hands worked the clay she held, fashioning it into the likeness of Abbot Bradford. There was something of the witch about the crone which drew them. They could smell her stink - unwashed body, stale cooking, half eaten food. Stains on her rough tunic were crusted with age. She embodied all that the twins relished. They listened as she outlined her next mischief and made their own plans.

Dionisia was frequently caught in her mischief and was no stranger to the Hundred Court. Neighbours were wary of her, kept their distance but were careful to keep on the right side of her. She was adept at setting neighbours one against the other with rumour, half -truth, sometimes downright lies. Now she was planning on some scandal which would make big news for the Abbot – not good news, either. She had been walking through Hound Street one early evening last year, pausing at open casements to listen and pry. She had overheard a juicy bit of information, half understood, which she had been following up since then. The couple had a son, now six Summers old, who, it appeared was supported by monies coming from an unknown source. That sounded extremely juicy to Dionisia, and she had watched and waited, crept near to windows, squirreled away snippets of knowledge waiting until she had enough to make sense of the thing. She knew that the couple had been childless and suddenly had the boy – but that was some six years ago. She had watched carefully as the couple were visited by the Coroner from time to time, but now she felt she had the key to the puzzle. Oh, how she would use it! The parents were not wealthy people. The mother took in sewing, there was only one other child, a girl and they were careful with their resources, yet the boy had started this trimester at Thomas Copeland's School in Sherborne. Was the Abbot paying his fees? How could a family such as that gain access to Thomas Copeland's school? Very fishy, Dionisia decided. Well worth digging some more.

As she watched the twins swagger away from her, she smoothed the last of her model of Abbot Bradford. Oh yes, the Abbot would certainly sing to her tune!

Sherborne was a busy place on this day. With a market in full swing the cobbled streets were filled with colour, noise, smells and animals, as well as people going about their daily grind. A wandering friar declaimed that heaven would fall if the wickedness of the earth did not cease forthwith;

the small crowd clustered around him laughed at his mincing gait and his reedy voice, straining to be heard above the clamour of the street cries. He had his pitch on the corner of Lodbourne, and old wives rested gladly there, hardly listening to him at all, but glad to rest before they climbed the steep incline of Cheap Street once more. Trade was in full swing on this late May morning, glovers, fletchers, weavers, bakers; the stench of the butchers from The Shambles overtook the more fragrant smell of the bakehouse and ladies of the town used pomanders as they trod carefully on the cobbles. Old Amelisia with her tray of fragrant herbs lovingly gathered and assembled while the dew was still on them was doing good business this morning, for the butchering was provoking some gut-wrenching smells, catching the throat unpleasantly.

A commotion at the top of the street caught her attention. She peered up the hill, squinting to see the cause. A rush of people; there was chaos and mayhem caused by squealing pigs, overturning stalls. Children were shouting, running in high excitement, tumbling over in their haste to catch some of the piglets running with the sows and boars, risking being over-run by this herd of escaped pigs, trotting, no, galloping totally out of control. They were nosing into stalls, shop fronts - Good Lord - however many of them? Where had they come from? Her old legs trembled as they drew nearer - men were throwing themselves frantically onto the running herd to try and catch them before the market was utterly decimated. Amelisia was unable to move fast enough. A fat, muddy young boar charged into her, knocking her to the ground, her herbs spoilt and trampled, her tray smashed as the brute moved on, leaving her in disarray on the ground, bruised and tearful.

Her careful work in ruins around her, Amelisia raised herself cautiously on one elbow, shuffling herself nearer to the wall to escape the onslaught of pigs as they streamed down the hill after their leaders, snorting and snuffling as they progressed. Men shouted, some successful in capturing the animals. Children screamed with excitement as they ran after the disappearing herd. Goodwives and mistresses joined the affray, scolding, screeching, attempting to rescue spilt goods before they were looted in the panic. Pot boys from ale houses ran outside to join the fun, eager to snatch a few minutes of excitement and grab a handful of broken fruit or pies. A visiting cloth merchant took pity on Amelisia and raised her to her feet, but her tray and her wares were past help. In despair, she limped painfully through The Shambles and onto the Abbey green, where she could rest for a few minutes before beginning her lonely walk home, coins ground into the mess left by the herd, tray destroyed, hope extinguished.

At the top of Cheap Street, the twins, well hidden, grinned at each other in delight. What a success! It had taken them some time to organize such a commotion, but with the willing help of friends, it was a huge success. Leave someone else to catch the beasts was their maxim – the sight of so many God-fearing citizens overturned, running before the galloping pigs, hats in the mud trampled by the herd, portly men, decorous wives, wide eyed apprentices all scrambling to protect their wares – oh what a delight!

CHAPTER THREE

The Abbot's boy

Luke had been bent to his lessons when the pigs made their wild bid for freedom, assisted by the twins' escapades. Master Copeland paused in his rhetoric and dismissed the boys, instructing them to assist the market traders and any others needing help. He was well aware that many ordinary folk would have been frightened, inconvenienced and even mildly hurt. He felt some compassion and assistance by the scholars would be appreciated.

The scholars emerged from their school at the bottom of Cheap Street and surveyed the chaos of the overturned market, fruit rolling down the cobbles, dung from the excited animals spoiling goods. Excited ragged arsed children were screaming with delight at the sight of upright citizens scrambling to stand upright and dust off their clothes if they had been knocked over by the rush, as several of the older ones had been. The guildmaster strode among the shattered stalls and scattered goods to prevent looting, for beggars were quick to take advantage of the unusual situation. Some anger among the townspeople was bubbling up already, and the guildmaster quickened his pace to arrive at the top of the street from where the pigs had emerged. His face darkened with anger at the mess and destruction of a valuable day's trading.

Sir Tobias emerged from his usual place of business, William at his side. His scribe was less bold; he remained inside the George Inn, fearful of animals on the rampage. In his experience, pigs could become vicious if restrained against their will, and he was not about to allow himself to be their victim.

The clamour of angry traders, distressed goodwives, excited children and the shouting of watchmen anxious to detect thieving made a cacophony of hell for a few minutes, the street regaining something approaching order as one or two of Master Copeland's released scholars pitched in to help restore the day's orderliness. Other scholars took the chance to follow the path taken by the retreating pigs, tearing after them in glad joyousness, thrilled at an unexpected release from the schoolroom.

Luke took a different path. He noticed the retreating back of Amelisia, limping through The Shambles, leaving her spoilt goods and broken tray on the ground where she had fallen. He knelt on the cobbles and scraped up some of her herb nosegays, crushed but still fragrant. He grubbed among the dirt and rescued one or two coins, then collected the broken pieces of her tray. Titus watched him, unwilling to stoop so low but not wanting to swoop after the other boys in their excited flight after the vanishing pigs. Luke followed the path Amelisia had taken, Titus following him at a distance. The stench from The Shambles made both boys quicken their pace through the narrow lane and they were glad when they emerged on the Abbey green.

They found Amelisia crouched on the ground before the Abbey, keening softly to herself. Titus drew closer to Luke, reassured by his friend's boldness at approaching her.

"Mistress, you left some coin behind," Luke murmured softly. She looked up fearfully, expecting a blow or kick.

"Some of your herbs might give you peace," Luke continued, holding them out to her. She extended a shaking hand and took them, drawing them in to herself as she would a baby.

"There are some parts of your tray, too." He put them on the ground before her but both he and Titus could see that they were too smashed for repair.

"The tray was my husband's last piece of work. Now he has gone I cannot repair it., but I thank you."

She mumbled her thanks through a split lip from her fall, the tears drying on her worn cheeks, her thin neck and tousled hair making a truly abject picture. Her black button eyes surveyed the two scholars warily as she took the coins from Luke and stood up, wincing at the pain from her grazed knees.

"Mistress, are you hurt?" Titus asked her. Luke looked in amazement at his friend. Could this be Titus, concerned about the old herb seller? He was surprised that Titus had followed him.

"No, no kind sirs – I do thank you for your kindness." She moved stiffly away, leaving the debris from her selling tray behind her. Luke gathered the pieces up and followed her as she trudged over the green, meaning to see her safely to her home. She turned suspiciously, anxious less these two scholars meant her harm, despite their soft words.

Luke anticipated her concern, and assured her that they were only making sure she reached her home with no further mishap but she was not willing to divulge her poor home to these well- meaning young scholars, - who knew what that might bring – and why would they want to walk where she had her abode – poor, broken down and squalid in comparison to their clean, neat apparel. She brushed them aside with a clear indication that she would not welcome their assistance any further. Luke understood, and the two boys watched as she hobbled on alone.

The cottars on the Northern edge of Sherborne were dismayed at the disappearance of their foraging pigs. Poor country dwellers, most households had several pigs, permitted to roam free, foraging for food during the Spring and Summer months before being fattened for meat. All pigs had to be ringed by Michaelmas, and then most families relied on the meat to tide them through the Winter months, together with the sale of fattened pigs nearer to Christmastide. The disappearance of pigs belonging to several families nearest to the town on the Northern edge caused consternation and despair. When they heard of the rush of pigs causing mayhem and destruction to the market in the town they were fearful of the penalties incurred for causing such a happening. They cowered in their cottages, wanting to shout out loudly about the loss of their animals but fearful of the consequences if they were blamed for the destruction of the market.

Daniel and Noah were unrepentant. What did they care for the loss of a few pigs? If the cottars wanted to get them back they could go to the Southern edges of the town and search for them. They would have come to rest somewhere.

They had indeed come to rest, although not all together. Some had found woodland, some had mingled with sheep belonging to the Abbot or the Bishop and some were muddying the waters of the river running by the castle. In all the twins and their cohort had driven some twenty animals to the top of the town, working separately with no more than three or four animals apiece driven by a sharp switch, and quite astonishingly had been observed by very few people. They had met at the top and simply thrashed the leader hard with their switches, and once one ran, they all followed, helter-skelter, snorting and squealing, grubbing out delicacies and overturning both stalls and people. The cohort had melted away, grinning, meeting on vacant pasture land, lying on their backs in the meadow, chortling over the success of their mischief.

Edmund, the Abbot's reeve, was not amused when he discovered three pigs snorting among a flock of the Abbot's sheep, causing the sheep to scatter. He drove them off to nearby woodland, leaving them snouting in the undergrowth happily, while he returned to his work. He heard about the confusion in the town and wondered where the remainder of the pigs were, but it was not his business to find them. Scowling, he returned to his tally sheets in the barn. He noticed the Jolif brothers had been struck off the tally, and paused to wonder. It would be like them to cause mischief. He would mention it to the bailiff.

The bailiff had already sought out Sir Tobias who was still in town, and was of the same mind as his reeve. The Jolif brothers were no longer working and might have cause for resentful mischief. Sir Tobias recalled the pair in his court just a day or two ago. He narrowed his eyes and considered. There had been no sign of them in the street — just pigs. Could it be chance?

"I will look into it, Bailiff," he promised.

Edmund took the first watch of the night himself. There were more sheep to be sheared by the itinerant shearers and he wanted the beasts to be all together to save time. It cost his lord much coin to have the shearing completed and they could not afford to waste time travelling from field to field, so Edmund had worked with his men all day, gathering the flock from each part of the demesne. Now he lay against a stone water butt, chewing on the coarse bread and dried bacon his wife had provided for his repast. The flock were quiet, no sound but the snuffle and rhythmic movement of their jaws, working the cud over and over before swallowing, then heads down, the noise of the sweet grass tearing as they searched out their next morsel. The night was black for the moon would not rise until much later but when he had finished his bread, he would rise and walk the vastness of this field, checking the perimeters and keeping himself awake.

His footsteps were quiet as he began his rounds of the flock, the night air warm and smelling of the cropped grass, damp earth and - yes, he was not mistaken - wood smoke. There was a fire burning in the near vicinity. He slowed his pace, nose upturned to catch the direction of the smell. He felt at his belt for his dagger, allowed his hand to remain on the hilt as he moved cautiously forward. His eyes strained to see further into the darkness and as he breasted the rise in the rough ground, he was able to see the red glow of a small fire, sparks rising in the air. Anger filled him at the thought of the brazen sauce of poachers who must surely be planning to cook their stolen meat in the very place of their theft. He drew nearer, silently, slowly watchful. A scuffle somewhere in the darkness, frightened bleating of a sheep, a shouted oath. He ran towards the fire, roaring in his rage at the discovery of more theft and desecration. several raised voices – chaos - figures emerged from the gloom, one brandishing a raised knife, dripping with gore from the freshly slaughtered sheep which Edmund could now hear clearly, gurgling unpleasantly in its death throes. He could make out very little in this darkened place, despite now being nearer the source of the fire.

Three men rushed him before he could draw his readied dagger, knocked him to the ground, kicked the fire, rolled him over, a fist met his mouth, a grunt and a curse...a final dagger thrust and they were gone, leaping over their fire leaving Edmund clawing the ground beneath him, bleeding heavily. He was aware of a vision of fit figures, lithe and young, but could not see faces in the dark with the light of the fire blinding his sight. He shuddered from the shock, attempted to stem the flow of blood with his own tunic and pulled himself away from the fire which had been scattered in the flight of the perpetrators. The last thought before he lost consciousness was that he would have to survive for several hours before the watch changed.

His own son discovered him, he who had agreed to take over from his father. Fourteen years old, anxious to earn himself a place in the team of workers, he stumbled over the inert body of his father lying near the spent scattered ashes of a small fire. The boy's first thought was to try and rouse his father, horrified that he had allowed himself to fall asleep when on watch for vandals. He shook his arm, then felt the congealed blood and drew back in shocked realisation. Edmund's body felt cold but there was slight movement of the chest, and the boy Tomas did the first thing which occurred to him, - he ran as fast as he could to the home of the bailiff, hammering on the door, now in a panic, forgetful of the midnight hour, the status of the bailiff, the wisdom of leaving his father lying still cold and unprotected.

The bailiff took his time to answer, sleepy and stiff in manner to begin with until he understood the attack and the consequence. He roused his man servant and together the men retraced the way Tomas had fled for help, Tomas now fearful that his father had died.

The sheep had moved away from that particular piece of pasture, the smell of slaughtered sheep's blood unsettling them, but Edmund lay motionless by the ashes, where Tomas had left him. Although now, Tomas noticed, he was covered with a thick black cloak, which had not been there before. This puzzled him, but there was no time to comment, and in any case he was somewhat in awe of the bailiff and his man, who were gentle with Edmund as they lifted him carefully onto a hurdle they had thought to bring with them.

"Your father lives yet," the bailiff told him, gruffly., as he bandaged the wound with cloth strips. "Makepeace will go for the barber surgeon at first light. You can stay with him if you wish...we can house him in the barn."

So Tomas spent the remainder of the night watching over his father, aware that he was still bleeding, although now slowed to a steady ooze, and the bailiff himself took over the watch with the flock, uncertain of how badly injured his reeve was.

Makepeace vanished to call the barber surgeon as dawn broke, and Tomas, by now thoroughly chilled himself, looked askance at his father's grey face, troubled by his shallow breathing and occasional groans of pain.

The surgeon, Master Jacobson, reached them as the bailiff's wife brought Tomas some watered ale with bread and cheese to break his fast. She expressed concern that her husband had left Tomas alone with his injured father, and had not thought to call the surgeon in the night. Tomas was only too relieved to see him now as he thanked the good woman for his food, wolfing it down, watching Master Jacobson remove the strange cloak and strip the tunic carefully away from the wound. It bled freshly as he did so, the oozing having congealed tackily during the chill of the night.

Once cleansed with wine and water, carried by the surgeon in his pack, the stitching needed to be done. Tomas followed the surgeon's instructions, although his stomach

31

felt distinctly uneasy as he watched, feeling his father's pain vicariously. Edmund had begun to regain consciousness as the stitching began, and Tomas found it hard to hold his father as instructed, and was relieved when the bailiff appeared to assist.

"The cost of the barber surgeon will be covered by me," he told Tomas, "and when he has woken and is able to walk, take him home. I will call on him to see what he can tell me. I think he has been lucky."

Edmund moved very cautiously, shaken by the stitching, aching from lying on the hard ground, still chilled from his night in the open but grateful to be alive. He was unwilling to keep the cloak, insisting that it was not his to keep, but the bailiff dismissed this as nonsense, adding that the warmth of this cloak had kept Edmund alive, and he could return it if he found an owner in due course. In the light of the circumstances, no-one thought to query where or how they had come by this cloak, but it was with a sense of relief that Edmund finally arrived at his own small home, and his wife, much gladdened to see him, merely hung the cloak on a peg near the door without comment, more worried by the injury and the pallor of her husband's face. There would be questions to answer in the forthcoming days, but for now, he was home, stitched and alive.

Three sheep were slaughtered that night, left in the fields where they lay, neatly sliced. The bailiff himself inspected the site in the light of the day, angry at the repeated slaughter, indignant at the attack on his reeve and amazed that anyone should be so brazen as to think of lighting a fire to cook meat as they killed. This had to stop. Before he left the site he stamped the remains of the fire out, anxious lest any hidden sparks should set off more desecration. He thought hard as he returned to the farm;

there had been much petty disturbance recently, and now it seemed to be escalating. Mostly it was damage to property of the Bishop, walls demolished left as heaps of rubble causing more work to repair, now sheep slaughtered in the field, left almost as a message for the Bishop, and even the Abbot. The number was increasing but more troublesome now was the attack on his reeve, Edmund, who had clearly come across the perpetrators and was unable to defend himself. He thought briefly on the thick cloak which had been laid across Edmund and which Edmund claimed did not belong to him, but he could find no explanation for it and dismissed the cloak from his mind.

Sherborne Castle was expecting Bishop Ayscough to reside for a short period before returning to Windsor, where the King held court at present. The King's recent nuptials were over and the Bishop had travelled to Salisbury and thence onwards to Sherborne, his normal place of residency during the infrequent periods he spent in his bishopric.

His bailiff was not looking forward to the ensuing interview with the bishop. It fell to him to explain the loss of sheep, the failure to apprehend any of the culprits and the attack on the reeve, Edmund. In addition to that there had been other incidents such as the firing of a deserted shack on his land, a fodder storage container broken open and wasted fodder spoiled by rain fall as a consequence. Lately there had been piles of waste soil and debris blocking paths, placed to deliberately hinder the trackway to the castle and the lanes surrounding it. All very vexatious.

The bailiff left the castle a little time later feeling most put upon by the arrogance and lack of understanding of the bishop. He was charged with working towards an end to the disruption and could offer no assistance to the reeve, who would be unable to work until recovered sufficiently.. enough to make him seek out some of the trouble makers and join them, he thought, as he strode down the hill towards his home. Perhaps after all the cloak might be a clue to the perperators – but who would have had the nerve to return to their scene of crime and cover a man they thought might be dead?

Dionisia settled herself down on a wall near the bottom of Cheap Street, with one eye on the door of Thomas Cope's school. As the morning wore on she gathered a small group of women round her, all gossiping about the sheep found slaughtered, the attack on the reeve, the flight of the pigs. Dionisia's hand tightened round her carefully made effigy of Abbot Bradford hidden in the folds of her dirty skirt as the door of the school opened to release some of the scholars for their break.

"Isn't that the Abbot's boy?" she commented innocently, hugging herself for her good luck in noticing the child as he emerged with several others.

"What?" cackled another crone, as she peered across the street at the group of youngsters.

"The Abbot's boy – look at him! Can't you see the resemblance? He's not as high and mighty as makes out, our Lord Abbot."

"No, that's the adopted child of Amice and her husband," a third voice volunteered.

Dionisia scoffed loudly, her gimlet eyes boring into the child opposite as the scholars clustered together, talking and laughing at some remembered misdemeanour.

"And where did that baby come from, I'd like to know? They had no luck for years....and suddenly there's money enough to send him to school, a quarry man and a seamstress, I tell you, the boy is the bastard of the Abbot." Her derisive chuckle was throaty, echoing across the street, as her sisters-in- gossip chortled along with her.

"Well now, what a thing, to be sure!" another cackled, "I'll tell my man, he'll be sure to know all the details."

"Now you mention it, he does look a bit like Abbot Bradford," another said, staring hard at the unfortunate lad. "It's the way the nose turns up, as if there's a bad smell under it."

"Now who's going to gain from this?" another commented, slyly, ever wanting a share in the gains; they knew Dionisia so well!

By nightfall the talk in the lesser ale houses was of the Abbot's bastard.

Dionisia was thrilled – it had been so easy to sow the seeds!

She called on Amice the next day. The house was clean, fragrant with herbs and Amice was working on fine sewing using light from the open window with late sun shining through. She answered the door herself, her sewing in her hands, needle thrust through the cloth to keep her place in the neatly embroidered motif.

She looked askance at her visitor but did not invite her in. Distrust and dislike were written on her homely face.

"Dionisia." She nodded in acknowledgement.

"Mistress Amice. Aren't you going to invite me in?"

"I hadn't considered doing so," Amice replied, tartly. Dionisia bridled – haughty bitch – she wouldn't be so hoity toity when she heard what Dionisia had come for.

"I would suggest you do just that. You wouldn't want our conversation to be overheard," Dionisia told her.

Amice's face darkened.

"Don't threaten me with the unknown, Dionisia. You are not welcome here."

Amice made to close the door but Dionisia was too quick for her.

"You would expose the boy to gossip then?"

"What invented trouble have you brought to my door, Dionisia?"

Amice blocked the entrance with her body, and as Dionisia attempted to push her out of the way Amice caught her thumb in the needle poking from the needlework, causing a drop of blood to appear and stain the work.

"Out of my house, gossipmonger!" exclaimed Amice angrily, shoving Dionisia so hard that she fell backwards, giving Amice room to slam her door in Dionisia's face.

Dionisia turned her ankle painfully in her effort to remain upright and spat viciously at Amice's door as she breathed heavily and limped back the way she had come, planning her next move. If Amice wouldn't co-operate, there were ways and means to force her, or there were ways to harm the Abbot himself. She would not be thwarted, so muttering incoherently to herself she re-entered her own hovel and drew out her effigy of Abbot Bradford, squeezing it hard in her hand as she searched for pins.

Meanwhile Amice's distress at the blood-stained garment she had been working on was more important to her than the ramblings of old Dionisia, known as a sly, deceitful scandal spreader. The work was commissioned by the wife of the goldsmith for her first granddaughter and was needed for the baptism shortly. Frustrated tears stung her eyes as she realised she would have to take the front out completely, re-cut and start the embroidery again – and fast. She gave no further heed to Dionisia's words, intent only on repairing the damaged work. That would prove to be a mistake.

CHAPTER FOUR

The Abbot's dilemma

Abbot Bradford knelt in prayer in his night shirt, plump hands clasped in front of him, eyes closed, knees protesting at his weight. However he was perceived by the townspeople, he took his responsibilities for the running of this great abbey very seriously. He was concerned for the welfare of all his household, both religious and layfolk. He cast his mind over the dealings he had with Sir Tobias, Coroner. It fell to him to provide Sir Tobias with the purse for Mistress Amice on a regular basis which for the last five years had been done privately, with no difficulty. More recently he had felt unease at snide comments from within the body of layfolk serving in the various departments of the abbey, made within his hearing, although sotto voce, as if he was meant to hear and be dismayed.

Prayers completed somewhat haphazardly, he raised himself from his knees with difficulty and paused at his glassed window, contemplating concerns about the monk who had placed him in this awkward situation. That affair had been dealt with five or six years ago, neatly disciplined, arranged privately with the Coroner....not a man he cared for, although he held him in a certain respect....Sherborne was fortunate in having an honest coroner, now also a Justice of the Peace.

Could it be that the brother in question, now older if not wiser, had attempted to see the child? He would be surprised if that were so. He would have expected to have received messages from the Abbot at Hyde Abbey if the brother had behaved foolishly. No mention had ever been made of the whereabouts of the child, - only he and the Coroner were aware. Abbot Bradford was not a man to doubt his capabilities, but he certainly felt an unusual sense of unease as he went about his duties. He clambered into his bed, crisp linen sheets, feather filled mattress and settled for sleep, but sleep eluded him. The whispers of the serving girl in the refectory returned to haunt him. She had been watching him as he stood for the final benediction after the meal, with a sly smile drifting over her plain face, more a sneer than a smile, and as she bowed her head during the benediction, he distinctly overheard the muttered "Mistress Amice looks after his child for money. What do you think of that?"

There had been more over the last few days, enough to cause concern. The abbot turned uneasily in the great bed, wondering whether he should confide in his prior. The affair, some five or six years ago, had been dealt with swiftly and very privately, the brother involved moved to Hyde Abbey, another Benedictine monastery, after due consultation with their Abbot.

The abbot had chosen to support the family who had taken the baby, aware that it was his responsibility to face his momentary lapse of discipline and care for the recalcitrant brother. It had been so satisfactorily dealt with that he hardly ever gave any thought to it, until now. What could be behind this, he wondered, aware that the sheets were tangling his legs uncomfortably as he turned yet again. How far would it go? Would it stop of its own accord? Suppose the Bishop heard the mutterings - no surely he would not be interested - Bishop Ayscough was hardly ever in the vicinity - he was much involved with the affairs of His Grace the king at court. Eventually his eyes closed, but sleep was fitful and disturbed. Perhaps he would seek an interview with Sir Tobias. There was no-one else he could speak to.

Sir Tobias was surprised to be invited to partake of wine with Abbot Bradford. It was hardly a friendship, nor even an amicable relationship. However, he responded with courtesy and at the appointed time found himself in the pleasant parlour of the house, built especially for the Abbot some few years ago. The house was slightly behind the main buildings of the Abbey and had an air of opulence hardly in keeping with the austerity of his calling. The buildings were of Ham stone, windows elegantly arched and suitably glassed. One was open to admit fresh air and the room smelled sweet with beeswax and lavender. Clearly the Abbot was well looked after.

Abbot Bradford was seated in his throne-like chair, carvings adorning the arms. A decorative oak table in front of him contained two silver goblets, jewelled on the stem. An aumbrey in the far corner of the room gave the room a feeling of a space for both work as well as leisure and a second carved chair near to the table had tapestried cushions on the seat to which he waved Sir Tobias. There was a crucifix on one wall, on the other walls were hanging tapestries depicting lives of saints. Despite the open window a small fire burned in the grate, logs emitting a pleasant smell adding to the beeswax and lavender. Altogether a most pleasing scene, despite the presence of the Abbot, Sir Tobias thought, wryly.

Diffident about beginning the conversation the Abbot edged round local affairs, asking the Coroner details of the sheep killings, the pig incident and sheep rustlings which were occurring with increasing regularity. The Coroner was bemused, wondering several times where this was all leading to. Eventually the Abbot took a deep breath; he could postpone the awkward conversation no longer.

"Sir Tobias, I have overheard murmurings from some of the lay persons in the Abbey which disturb me." He did not meet the Coroner's eyes as he spoke, most unusual for such an arrogant and often angry man. He continued, "they concern Mistress Amice and the child... now older by some five years."

"Doing very well with the family, I believe. I visit them as we arranged. They have put the purse to good use."

"So I understand. Coroner, you have not mentioned this to any other person over the years?" His eyes finally sought the Coroner's own. Sir Tobias saw a troubled man, anxious perhaps for his own position, a man who would seek to hide from public disdain, a man who had taken a responsible stand some years ago on behalf of a wayward brother under his leadership and who had not expected it to return to lay shame and blame at his own door.

"The rumours are circulating amongst your lay staff? Rumours which suggest that the boy belongs to you?"

The Abbot nodded, chin resting on his hand leaning on the table in front of him.

A little of his bombastic attitude returned as he felt the release of tension now he had revealed the true purpose of the visit.

"This is a preposterous situation for myself and the Abbey generally. Who has this information? How did it escape and become so convoluted and inaccurate? The brother involved is now at a distant monastery and could have no possible contact with any persons here in Sherborne. Has Mistress Amice spoken out to any companions?"

"I will visit her and enquire of both herself and her good husband, but I feel sure the answer will be negative. They live quietly, are hard -working and feel very blessed. Are you aware that after adopting the babe she and her husband did conceive and a healthy child was born to them...so they have two children now. I very much doubt that gossip of any description came from that household."

The Abbot was silent for a moment. He was unaware of the circumstances of Mistress Amice and her family; indeed, he had not met her, would not know her if they passed in the street.

"I would be grateful for your help in this matter, Sir Tobias. A discreet call on the family might be advisable, but I do not know how to still the gossip among the lay persons. Soon it will reach the brothers, and my position as their father Abbot will be compromised."

It was the turn of Sir Tobias to be silent. He did not feel it was his task to ferret among the lay persons in the Abbey, and there was a goodly number of them in many different walks of life he remembered from an earlier affair in which he had been involved.

"You would do well to discuss the matter with your prior. I know you have kept this incident entirely to yourself, Abbot Bradford, but two pairs of ears and eyes are better than one here. I urge you to speak to Prior William as a matter of urgency. I will call on Thomas Copeland to have very private words with him, and also Mistress Amice. Together we will do what we can, but it is a difficult situation which may simply need to run its course."

The Abbot sighed as he rose to see Sir Tobias out; this was not what he had hoped for, but he could understand the delicate nature of the business.

Neither Abbot Bradford nor Sir Tobias were aware of the listener under the open window crouched and hidden by bushes. As the voices drifted away, Dionisia stretched her cramped limbs and clambered out of the bushes – she grinned in pleasure, the knowledge that she had alarmed the Abbot was pleasing to her.

Sir Tobias allowed several days to pass before he called on Mistress Amice. She was working on some plain linen for the alms-house this day. Sir Tobias was mindful to be diplomatic, wary of causing her alarm. She was not expecting him. She put down her work and called to her little maidservant to bring watered ale for the Coroner. Her eyes were anxious as he tasted the ale and declared it acceptably good. He tried to put her at ease by asking after the boy. He had some knowledge of Thomas Copeland's school, for Luke was a pupil as had Matthias been.

"Is he in trouble with the Master?" she enquired, a frown knitting her features.

Sir Tobias assured her that he was not, that he had heard he was making good progress.

"He is described as your son?" the Coroner asked.

"Oh, yes, my lord, that is what we agreed," she nervously asserted, wondering to where this was leading.

"And no-one outside this house knows any differently?"

"Certainly not, my lord."

"You are absolutely sure of that?"

Mistress Amice twisted her hands together nervously.

"My lord, why are you asking me these things? My husband and I regard the boy as our own. We have had him since he was about two days old...no-one has ever questioned me, even though I gave no signs of being enceinte. No midwife came near me and yet I had the child. We keep ourselves very much to ourselves. It was accepted at the time that the babe was not mine – how could it be – but no-one asked, no-one was inquisitive and over the years the circumstances of his arrival appear to have been forgotten, especially as I quickened with child soon after his arrival and gave birth to a healthy little girl." Her face softened as she mentioned the girl, blushing at her temerity in making such a long speech to Sir Tobias.

Sir Tobias had no better luck when speaking with Thomas Copeland. The schoolmaster did not know the origin of the child, and Sir Tobias did not find it necessary to inform him. However, Thomas admitted that he was aware of a slight increase of interest from one particular troop of harridans who plied their trade at the bottom of Cheap Street most days. He noticed that they watched for the scholars to emerge whence they then pointed fingers at several of the youngsters, but in particular the son of Amice...called Arnet. The boy was a pleasant looking child with a friendly attitude so Thomas had thought nothing of it. However, now Sir Tobias had made him aware, he resolved to watch more closely as the boy was the youngest under his care.

He was dismayed when the very next day he watched as one of the street sellers gossiped with Dionisia, a known trouble maker. Raucous laughter emanated and he distinctly heard the phrase "Abbot's boy" tossed carelessly between them. He was thoughtful as he re-entered his dwelling to begin afternoon school.

Sir Tobias was alarmed at the extent of petty disturbances happening in and around Sherborne. The pig incident had started the trail, followed by the sheep slaughter, and more seriously the attack on the Bishop's reeve. He had made little progress with discovering the perpetrators. He had little hope of arresting any one person for this. He had made enquiries as to the whereabouts of the Jolif twins on the night of the attack but no-one had seen them for several days. It appeared they were lying low. That in itself was suspicious. The town had become quarrelsome, petty and distrustful. Sir Tobias privately blamed the Abbot's insistence on the payments demanded from the townspeople towards the rebuilding of the damaged Abbey. Progress was slow and the Abbot was in a state of constant aggression towards the populace.

He sought a meeting with the Bishop's bailiff to learn more concerning the attack on Edmund, but the man could tell him little more than was already known. Sir Tobias mentally marked the Jolif brothers down for the incident; However, he had no possible leads as to any others.....there was so much unrest in and around the town. Before he left, the bailiff mentioned the strange cloak which had been found covering his reeve – could this help to discover the identity of the attackers? The Coroner left, promising him that he would call on Edmund the reeve himself to see whether he was able to recall any further details and to look at the cloak, although he was sure that one cloak would be pretty much like any other cloak.

On his return he passed Thomas Copeland's school; leaning against the house opposite were the Jolif brothers. He considered speaking with them; they appeared to be watching the school house, but he was aware that simply watching, or appear to be watching was no reason for questioning. It was too early for the scholars to be released for a break in their studies but on reflection he decided to send William, who was in their usual room at The George, down to observe. William's observation disturbed the Coroner sufficiently to send him to Thomas Copeland again before riding home. William reported that the Jolif boys had stayed until the scholars were released, and had attempted to join in with a game they were playing. On being pressed further, William thought that one of the scholars was very young. That sounded like Mistress Amice's boy, Sir Tobias felt. Perhaps he would have to explain the relationship more fully to William and Thomas Copeland. It seemed the child was being watched.

Sir Tobias felt a frisson of disquiet, remembering Luke's experiences years ago. It would not do to ignore this situation, a problem indeed. Sir Tobias was ever mindful of the advice given to him as a young soldier by his captain.... don't talk of problems... talk of solutions. He bent his mind to this adage as he rode home, and by the time he was at Purse Caundle, he had a possible solution.

The Jolif brothers lounged up the hill towards Dionisia's place, kicking at wayward hens by the rough track, leering at a serving wench so hard that she stumbled against the wall, frightened by their groping hands. They released her with coarse laughter, neither of them interested in sexual encounters at this time. Dionisia was squatting outside her hovel, stirring something greasy and uninviting in a cracked cooking pot. The boys spread themselves on the ground beside her, inviting her to regale them with tales of mischief, but Dionisia was strangely unwelcoming today, muttering feverishly to the contents of the pot. They had nothing of any importance to tell her other than that they had positioned themselves near the school and had made audible comments, although in truth, neither of the twins were quite sure at which child the comments should be aimed, so they had simply been loud as they kicked around on the edge of the scholars. In this matter, they were amused at Dionisia's plans, but they were happy to do as she asked.

Dionisia was thinking fast after her encounter with Mistress Amice. She had her greedy avaricious eyes on the prize.....a fat purse for her silence from that haughty Abbot. Now, how best to proceed? The Abbot had been concerned enough to send for that fat Coroner. She had listened to as much of their conversation as she had been able to hear clearly. She stirred her pot so vigorously that some of the greasy contents slopped over her torn petticoats but she ignored the mess, hardly aware of it. She narrowed her eyes, focussing on a distant point towards the Abbey. What should she do next? She had the information that would damage; how could she use it to stir the Abbot to frightened action?

CHAPTER FIVE

The Coroner's solution

John Coker did not welcome the sight of Dionisia loitering outside his house. He knew her as a village gossip, a teller of tales and a dangerous enemy to make. His involvement in the sheep slaughtering and his presence when Edmund met his accident was something she had wind of, but he knew not how. She had waylaid him in his place of trading the day before, beckoned him out of hearing of his apprentice and asked a favour of him in exchange for her silence. Initially he had refused so she had told him she would seek him out again when he had time to consider her simple request.

He was a weaver, with increasing trade in the town, a small shop front displaying cloth, a place weekly in the markets around and was beginning to prosper. His wife and two daughters enjoyed the increasing prosperity and little bits of luxury that were starting to enter their lives. He certainly did not want Dionisia snouting around his life. How on earth had she come by the information? The conversation had been mildly unpleasant. She knew he was part of the sheep rustling group, that he had been privy to the killing of five of the Bishop's flock and had been present when Edmund the reeve was knifed. Maybe, she hinted slyly, he had wielded the knife? All she asked in return was a little gossiping among his friends….and then her silence would be assured.

John was not a stupid man; he doubted that would be the end of the affair. There would be more. His common sense told him that he should go to the bailiff and admit his part in the sheep killings, but he knew he could not do that. He would be the only suspect in the attack on the reeve. Why had Edmund surprised them so quickly? It did not give them time to think or act and so one of their number had jumped him, knife out and Edmund had run straight onto the blade, with unfortunate results. They had not intended it to end that way, and their silence was very important – so how on earth had Dionisia learned of it? He groaned softly, opening the door to meet her at the gate. Since as a group they intended to keep up their persistent goading of the Bishop and the Abbot, both of whom had such power in the town, he knew he would have to meet her suggestions, although he was doubtful of the truth in her reasoning.

His Grace King Henry and his Queen Margaret were visiting Glastonbury. The Abbot glared at the missive on his desk, sent by the Abbot of Glastonbury, extending an invitation to him to join them for the splendid visit. He was aware that wherever the royal personages travelled, a huge entourage followed them. The court would expect hospitality, entertainment, Masses…..an expense for the people of Glastonbury. His Grace had licenced the alms-houses in Sherborne some years previously – he felt his usual anger bubbling in him as he thought how fast the alms-house had progressed compared with the rebuilding of his damaged Abbey. He swallowed, striving to curb his resentment towards the willingness of the townspeople to donate to the alms-houses and how slowly they were raising the money he was demanding towards the fire damaged Abbey. And the battle of the font was not over yet, either. There was still no font in the chapel of ease, All Hallows. Baptisms were still held in the main Abbey, much to the disappointment of the common people of Sherborne. He would refuse the invitation to Glastonbury.

He left his house to return to the main Abbey, crossing through the Abbey garden, glancing up at the men on the scaffolding busy on the rebuilding. He could hear laughter as he approached, one voice clearer than the others exclaiming to another, "there goes Father Abbot – more father than you think!"

He felt cold as he swallowed and refused to raise his eyes to the scaffolders, pretending he could not possibly have heard them. Whatever was happening to him?

Sir Tobias visited Matthias and Alice as the scholars ended their afternoon. Matthias' man Davy always saw to their safe homeward journey and dealt with the horses, so there was time for him to play with his two young granddaughters, the apple of his eye. His pride in Luke's achievements were great but his relationship with these two little girls was something different altogether. They were very like their mother to look at, silky hair, creamy complexioned and sweet natured. Rose, the younger of the two was toddling behind Matthias as he emerged from the schoolroom and staggered towards her grandfather as he dismounted. He gathered her up in his arms and sat her on his great horse, chuckling at her excitement. Betony, now four, was more serious and watched as her sister patted the horse from her position high in the saddle.

Alice watched her father with affection. His face was weary, hot and troubled, and her heart lurched as she realised that he was looking old and rather tired. The petty troubles of the neighbourhood exhausted his resources although the neighbourhood watch were mostly honest hardworking men of the tithings. Over the last few years since being appointed a justice of the peace he had worked harder, seen more petty felonies and attracted some cases which had resulted in hangings, a not uncommon thing although far less than in the bigger cities. There were both stocks and a gibbet in Sherborne, neither used as frequently as bigger cities – Sherborne was still a quiet, gentle country town, despite the present disturbances.

Matthias lifted Rose down from the horse and hugged her tightly and Sir Tobias swept Betony to him in a bear hug. She giggled as his face tickled hers, hairy whiskers against her smooth skin.

"Will Luke be home this weekend?" the Coroner asked, as Alice led them into the house.

"No, - he has another week to go before he can come again. He was here two weeks ago quite animated about the pigs in the market place., and anxious to remake a tray for a seller of herbs whose work was smashed by the pigs. He can be such a thoughtful child."

"That sounds like Luke. I wonder if he will seek her out to give it to her when he has completed it? The pigs and the sheep rustlings pose just another problem for the Bailiff and the watch captains. Matthias, can I have a private word?"

Matthias followed his father-in-law into the schoolroom, deserted now. Alice took the girls with her into the house, carrying Rose on her hip comfortably. Matthias' eyes followed them warmly as she went to prepare wine and sweetmeats for her father when he had completed his business with Matthias. She wondered what task Matthias was to be involved with...she knew her father too well to suppose it was nothing of importance.

The Coroner perched on one of the trestles in the schoolroom, testing it cautiously for his weight before settling comfortably. He loved the smell of this room; Matthias had made a success of his school over the last five years, and the room was well organized, smelled of inks, parchment, beeswax, lavender, all overlaid by the sweat of the boys who were tutored by Matthias in this room. It had a lazy comfort, a business-like formality, an informal friendliness. The ambience was contradictory and he enjoyed being here with Matthias. He felt his weariness recede.

"What is it, father-in-law?" Matthias asked, leaning against his lectern, a newly made piece of equipment which he had commissioned from Martin Cooper, his friend and some-time lodger. It enabled him to stand in front of his scholars and retain any notes he needed in front of him, or to rest a precious book or scroll without the necessity to over handle it. Matthias had a huge respect for his tools, scrolls and books being a valuable commodity.

"Might you be able to take an extra child who may need temporary protection?" The Coroner came straight to the point. He was not a man to beat about the bush.

"Whose child?"

"The son of Mistress Amice, a seamstress in Sherborne."

"Why does he need protection?" Matthias knew he would not refuse this request, mindful of Luke's terrible experiences years ago, but he must discover the reason for the need, - he had his own family to protect if there was any danger. He was no longer a single man with no responsibility.

"This information is and must be confidential, Matthias. The child was born to a local girl and was sired by a brother from the Abbey who is unknown to me and who I now understand from the Abbot is lodged in a monastery some distance from here. The babe was deposited with the Abbot by angry relatives of the girl and the Abbot begged me to help find a place for the child. Mistress Amice and her husband had tried without success for a child of their own....Dame Goffe assisted me in this matter. The child has flourished and is supported financially by the Abbot... She has been receiving the purse with no problem for over five years." He paused for breath.

Matthias listened; this was surely a testament to the diminishing morals of some religious houses. He had in the past seen Abbot Bradford at his worst....now perhaps he was seeing another side to his leadership of the Abbey. What a pity it could not extend to the unification of town and Abbey, resolving the damaging disputes.

Matthias said as much to Sir Tobias.

"I'm not sure that the local disturbances are all to do with the font and the fire," the Coroner replied, "there have been many such disturbances up and down the country, fuelled by the politics of our young King, who, if the truth be told, is allowing the country to be ruled by noblemen around him, led by William de la Pole, earl of Suffolk. I met him, you know, Matthias, when I was searching for Luke. He has a considerable influence with His Grace, - an able man but I fear he is playing with fire. There are too many who jostle for position until our queen provides us with a son for Henry. The duke of York is one such....but that doesn't concern the present problem here in Sherborne. There are unpleasant rumours circulating in the Abbey which appear to be spreading into the town, that the boy is the son of the Abbot himself."

"Are you certain that he is not so?"

"I am certain. The Abbot would not dissemble with me. I remember well our conversation when he brought the

52

problem to me...he was humbled by the knowledge that his discipline of the brothers was not as it should be. Yes, I am certain the child is not the offspring of Abbot Bradford."

"How old is the child, and what makes you feel he needs protection?"

"The boy, Arnet, is the youngest pupil of Thomas Copeland. Of late the scholars have been watched as they emerge to take their leisure. Comments have been heard about "the Abbot's boy". Two of the town's most troublesome twins have picked him out for observation, trying to engage with him. Most recently, the Abbot himself has overheard the abbey labourers gossiping among themselves, declaring the child is fathered by him. I would like to remove the boy for a time from Sherborne until I have more news of how we can put a stop to this insidious slander."

"I would not be able to house him, as Thomas boards his scholars. Even with Luke away, I cannot offer him that kind of protection; it was partly the difficulty of seeing me as a schoolmaster during the day but a family man at home which caused confusion in Luke. I would not be happy for that to happen again."

The two men were silent for a space, thoughtful. Matthias spoke first.

"I am willing to have him as a scholar – I would not feel happy to refuse help in these times which seem to be beset with so much small unpleasantness, but he would need to lodge elsewhere – or travel daily."

Travelling daily was not an option for Arnet, - a child from a household of limited means, the family did not own horses, and had possibly not left the vicinity of Sherborne ever. Matthias agreed to think over the proposition and consider what might be put in place to help.

"May I discuss this with Alice?"

"I rely on her utmost discretion, but if it brings a conclusion, I would be grateful."

Sir Tobias must now return to speak with Mistress Amice before the plan could be put in place.

Matthias and Alice sat comfortably in their solar, Rose and Betony fed, settled, happy, ready for sleep. The day was coming towards its normal close, a time for this household to unwind after a day of work. Matthias loved his scholars, watched their progress with pride but wished there were more opportunities for these sons and daughters of local small merchants and tradesmen to progress further. Education was a costly business but it opened so many doors. Alice watched his face in the gathering gloom, loving every expression which passed over him. She had come to value the relative simplicity of her life here. Once she had felt threatened by the drop in her status; now remembering that time she still felt traces of shame that she had not recognized the wholesome nature of Matthias' chosen path. It was due to him that she had found in herself the love of teaching her young charges, and had developed into a good business woman, running the details of the school when Matthias gave occasional assistance to her father.

"What was Father's purpose in his visit today?" she asked. She knew she would receive an honest answer, for they had no secrets from each other since the days of Luke's ordeal. Alice had steeled herself then to face life without her son and as a widow for the second time. It had made them both so much stronger.

Matthias explained the circumstances to her carefully, making her aware of his need to protect a child who might be as vulnerable as Luke had been but the necessity to keep his own family from any kind of close involvement.

"No harm to any one of us," Matthias declared, firmly, stroking Alice's face gently as he drew her to him, always experiencing the tug of desire as she pressed herself towards him. They stayed thus for a few seconds before Matthias gave in and led her to their bedchamber.

After their lovemaking, she lay in Matthias' embrace, content but her mind turning over the conversation regarding Arnet's situation.

"How would it be if he lodged with Martin and Lydia?"

Matthias was half asleep, satisfied and pleasantly weary. "Who?"

"Arnet. Lodging with Martin and Lydia?"

Matthias raised himself on one elbow and looked down on her face. How like her, he thought, to still be ferreting at the problem, despite her own peaceful state of mind.

"They would not have room, I think. Martin would agree and Lydia would worry."

"Then what about Ezekiel and Martha? They are good people and they would have room...and Arnet could travel to school with the boys."

"Mmm...maybe that's the answer....when I've completed tomorrow's work I'll call on him."

She drew him down for a last lingering kiss and caress before falling into sleep once more.

The Jolif twins were happy to be the ears and eyes for Dionysia, despite their amusement in her plan. She paid them a penny or two, and as they had no other work, that suited them. They hung around the street, lounging on walls, leering at maidservants as they went about their work and generally made themselves an unpleasant nuisance.

Dionisia planned her campaign against the Abbot, hugging to herself all the snippets of information she thought she had gathered over the last year. She was adept at listening at doors and windows, sliding into shadows to overhear conversations and planting doubt in the minds of others. She was disappointed that she had not been able to frighten Mistress Amice, but there were other avenues she could explore....and the boys were working hard for her, watching the young boy whom she was now convinced was the son of the Abbot himself.

Unknown to Dionisia, another hooded watcher was also interested, listening at windows, stalking the child, hungry for information. He noticed the twins several times as he gnawed on his lip anxiously wondering what their purpose was. He turned away to purchase a pie from a seller further down the street, and by so doing, missed the Coroner's squire collecting Arnet from the school, riding away in the direction of Milborne Port.

Sir Tobias had not found it easy to convince Mistress Amice that it would be better for Arnet to be away from Sherborne for a short while for his own safety. She and her husband demurred, procrastinating in their decision until Sir Tobias thought they would never reach the right decision, but mention of Luke's experience some years previously finally made their minds up, and Arnet was collected by William, who took him to Milborne Port, mounted in front of him. Arnet was wide eyed with wonder as they rode out of Sherborne, a little in awe of William, but full of questions as they made their way towards Milborne Port.

Matthias had made satisfactory arrangements for Arnet to stay with the barber surgeon and his family, travelling in to school each day with Ezekiel's boys, who were still with Matthias' school. Ezekiel agreed to take him with no prying questions. His sons were older than Arnet but friendly, nearing the end of their time with Matthias.

Dionisia was puzzled by the non-appearance of the child over the next few days. The twins grew lazy and bored with their watching brief and fell by the wayside, consorting with their dubious group of friends in the Gooseberry ale house. The ale at the Gooseberry was pale and rather thin, lacking in flavour but it was what the boys could afford; they were tolerated by the somewhat lacklustre ale keeper and welcomed by the pot girl who enjoyed their groping fingers every time she passed, which was as often as she could manage. The greasy walls closed them in, making a dreary setting for any but the lowest of society, earthen floor scuffed, tables broken and stained. Tinkers frequented the place, pickpockets congregated there to share out their "earnings", the pot girl was not averse to taking customers into a back room to sell her services to anyone willing to part with a few coins and the place reeked of stale onions, urine and animals. The boys knew they would have to go back to Dionisia, otherwise they would have no coin at all, even for this wretched place.

Dionisia continued to be mystified by the absence of the child when the scholars ran outside for a welcome break at midday. She was annoyed that she had apparently lost the help of the two pesky brothers who used her for whatever they chose. She grumbled to her neighbours in the street, but there was no sign of the youngest child today, so she trudged round to the house of Mistress Amice to discover whether the brat had fallen ill.

The house was closed, no windows open and no sign of Mistress Amice. A neighbour, recognizing Dionysia, informed her that the seamstress was out delivering work and that the child had accompanied her. Dionysia had forgotten temporarily that the little girl would have been at home, assumed that the child mentioned was the boy and searched the streets for some time for the pair before giving up in temper. The neighbour regretted giving the information as soon as her mouth opened, and watched as Dionisia turned the corner, vowing to mention the visit on the return of Mistress Amice.

Meanwhile John Coker and his cohort of irritants to the Abbot and Bishop had lain low for a number of days following the untimely wounding of Edmund the Reeve. It really had happened as John Coker had discussed with the chastened group of men; Edmund had surprised them so suddenly in his anger at their blatant killing of sheep and the insolence of actually daring to cook and celebrate in the Abbot's fields, that he had run onto the knife which one of the men had drawn, holding it ready to use if needed. They regretted the incident but did not dare to confess; now he was tortured with the knowledge that there had been another sheep killing in the fields that same night and somehow the old crone had been told that he had been involved. Someone in that other group must have caught sight of them. What was he to do? How long would she hold her spiteful tongue? How many more times would she ask for favours....and what was she up to? The men all knew who had drawn the knife but in their loyalty had agreed that the name would not pass their lips. But for the sake of the oppressed citizens of Sherborne, striving against the inequalities of the petty laws and the coming breakdown of law and order further along the coast, they determined to continue their irritations and the next planned disobedience was appealing to their sense of humour as well as the inconvenience to the Abbey.

CHAPTER SIX

A fishy interlude

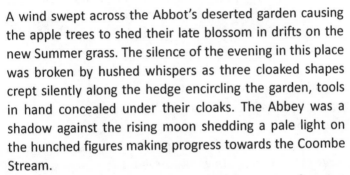

A wind swept across the Abbot's deserted garden causing the apple trees to shed their late blossom in drifts on the new Summer grass. The silence of the evening in this place was broken by hushed whispers as three cloaked shapes crept silently along the hedge encircling the garden, tools in hand concealed under their cloaks. The Abbey was a shadow against the rising moon shedding a pale light on the hunched figures making progress towards the Coombe Stream.

To their right was the drainage ditch; every so often one of the men would pause to grapple with the hurdles placed strategically in the ditch and wrench it from its place discarding it carelessly in the vegetation. The Coombe stream, clear fresh water, fed the Abbot's fish pond well stocked with perch, roach and an abundance of eels. The fish pond was not as large as some other abbeys, being some three quarters of an acre and oval in shape, fringed with trees. Being small and needed chiefly to provide fish for the Abbot and monks and occasionally to send fresh fish to other holdings of the Abbey, there was just one fisherman employed by the Abbey who managed the supply, oversaw the stock and sometimes needed to employ men to fish the pond when any festivities were expected.

On this night, as on many others, he was enjoying a blackjack of ale in his favourite ale house, safe in the knowledge that the small fish pond was secure...sometimes poached by local men but he turned a blind eye to that.... who wouldn't, when the Abbot was demanding such payment from his fellow townsmen?

The wind quickened as they approached the drainage area. The surface of the water ruffled in the breeze, lapping the edge of the reeds grown up around the edges. The hurdles preventing the fish from escaping had been removed on their way; they now stood together anticipating this next great mischief. The quiet plop of a surfacing fish broke the silence; they were aware that many fish swam in these waters, carefully bred for the community of the Abbey. The townspeople expected to see little of the harvest – these ponds were for the communities of monks and other churchmen ...it was the same throughput the land...many fish ponds belonging to bishops and abbots were bigger but they all served the same purpose, Sherborne was no different. The difference was in the punishment imposed by the Abbot on the people of Sherborne for the great fire....a heavy debt to pay, which he insisted on rubbing in to their collective noses. The bishop's croukpenny tax on their ale was still added to their drinking pleasures, too....and Bishop Ayscough was certainly not proving to be any help to their arguments with Abbot Bradford. They had all heard of the continuing unrest in other Southern shires further along the coast and whilst their grievances were far more local, the stories told by tinkers and travelling merchants of deliberate provocations were fuelling their actions.

Richard Vowell and Thomas Hoddinotte knelt on the wet grasses by the side of the drain. Richard gazed out across the water, the weak moon shining on the surrounding quiet sedges. A deep breath from both of them as their third companion, John Cocker, stood watching them. Were they going to pull the drainage or would they refuse at the last minute? Draining this pond was a deliberate act of disobedience, a scurrilous act against Abbot Bradford. The fish would be swept down the drainage channels to the Coombe stream which eventually fed the River Yeo....the rush of water would flood the Abbey garden and possibly Acreman Street....and many fish would die as the water drained. John Cocker remembered how somehow they had been seen as they slaughtered the sheep when the Reeve was injured....had anyone followed them? He stared out intently over the way they had trod....he could see no movement in the track beside the hedgerows from where they had crouched and moved so carefully. He recalled the gossip Dionisia had implored him to spread....what mischief was she up to? He dismissed it from his mind....she was no more than a gossiping troublemaker. This draining of the fish pond would make Abbot Bradford take notice of the anger of the town; he could see no reason why they should stop now, - the hurdles were removed, they had crept like thieves into the precinct of the pond and were ready to do the deed. There was no better time than now. He grasped his mattock impatiently and wrenched aside the side of the drain nearest to him, pushing his two companions aside. If they were hesitating, he most assuredly was not. The drain was stuck hard, embedded into the bank of the neck of the bank. He put all his strength behind the tool and bit by bit he felt it give. Richard realised they could not turn back now. He leapt over the ditch and using his own tools grappled with the drain from the other side. It gave with a sucking noise, and initially nothing happened as the three men watched expectantly, and then the swell of water began, escaping down the drainage ditch, fish swirling with the rushing water. It continued at a pleasingly fast rate without seeming a raging torrent. The men couldn't resist dipping their hands in and easily catching wriggling fat perch for themselves and their families. Wrapping their catches in their cloaks and waiting until the dying squirms of the fish had stilled to a mere twitching, the three straightened up, and with fresh fish wrapped securely in their dripping cloaks, they began their return journey as silently as they had come. Beside them they could see in the moonlight the now overfilled drainage ditch flowing swiftly with muddy water which would surely flood the Abbey garden on its way down to join the stream - some fish would live - more would die, gasping and wriggling in the eventual muddy silt of the fish pond. How many would be saved depended on when the fisherman returned to the place – he did not necessarily go every day, so it might not be discovered for a day or two. A satisfactory night of disruption they all agreed as they slipped cautiously into their own houses, agreement that no word of this be uttered and secure in the knowledge that this time they had not been observed.

The Abbot was indeed furious when the draining of the fish pond was discovered late the following day. The swell of water had caused Lodbourne to flood, and when lay persons from the Abbey had trudged up to the fish pond they understood what had caused the mud, silt and smelly water lying in the street at Lodbourne, and the thick mud overlying parts of the Abbey garden were unpleasant, especially as there were several dead stranded fish some still gasping at their gills...the monks gathered these up to deliver to the kitchen but in dismay rather than delight.

The Abbot sought his bailiff in anger, demanding that the miscreants be found, but his anger increased ten-fold when Sir Tobias called to inform him that the flooding of Lodbourne was in his tithing and would incur a fine. He was apoplectic and demanded that the Coroner should walk up to the site of his fish pond to survey the extent of the damage.

Sir Tobias folded his arms as he arrived at the site, indeed a sorry sight. There was a small amount of water remaining in which one or two smaller fish were struggling to survive. The muddy area around the drain itself yielded no clues as to the perpetrator, having been trampled by the bailiff and the woebegone fishpond reeve – the fisherman. The grating of the drain itself had been replaced, and the broken hurdles had been collected up and were being replaced by new ones, but the overall extent of the damage was chiefly in the loss of the fish stock and the flooding caused by the event. The Abbot and his prior were tight lipped with rage at this afront to their property. The restocking and refilling of the fishpond would cost them good silver….a purchase from a vivarium to restock…days to refill and strengthen and repair the drainage ditch, and the insult of the fine for the flooding of Lodbourne was more than the Abbot could tolerate, but Sir Tobias pointed out coolly that the fault lay with the Abbey for not protecting their fishpond securely and the flooding would be dealt with in the next hundred court hearing, when the Abbey would be fined according to the law. Abbot Bradford seethed. As if things weren't troublesome enough at the moment with this false rumour being circulated among the lay persons on his staff - he was determined to seek out the mischief makers and see them hanged.

Finn raised his head from his laboured scriving in Alice's room to watch the new arrival copying with such ease that

Finn felt quite jealous. He had felt he still needed extra practice with his forming of letters and words and had asked to remain with Alice for just a little longer, and Alice was happy to have him there for an hour each day to afford him the practice he needed. Arnet was a little bewildered by the sudden changes which had overtaken him, but he was an obedient child and had settled well with the Jacobsons, Daniel looking after him like a true older brother. It was an unusual experience for Arnet to travel to school mounted in front of Master Jacobson, the other two boys following on their own mounts. He had not been taught by a woman previously, but he was too young to feel astonished by that. Mistress Barton seemed lively and interesting – more so than the rigours of Master Copeland's more formal school.

He had seen little of Master Barton, who taught mostly the older boys, and Finn was normally in that upper group of scholars. Arnet was a little scared of the way Finn watched him working, but when Finn realised the child was aware of him, he gave a smile which reassured Arnet.

Matthias was pleased with how well the arrangement had settled – Ezekiel reported very little trace of concern, and his own boys had taken to the changes quite well. Matthias hoped the unfounded gossip round the Abbot would fade out quickly to enable Arnet to be restored to Thomas Copeland's school.

Dionisia stood perplexed for several days.....she returned time and time again to the bottom of Cheap Street and was furious at the apparent disappearance of Arnet. The Jolif brothers seemed to be intent on another course of action and she had to track them down where they unwillingly agreed to seek out the whereabouts of the boy.

Dionisia meanwhile took herself to the home of Amice once more, seeking a way to spy on the back entrance. She squeezed herself round to the small yard which gave access to the local shared privy. She was surprised to realise that one of the lay stalls was occupied....silently....and for some time. She slid round the side of the construction to where she could peer through the slats to observe who had need to occupy the stall for so long. Grinning sourly to herself she squinted through the crack to discover another listener.... not seated on the latrine seat.....just silently standing with his eye pressed against the door from where he could presumably watch the comings and goings.

She watched him for a while, becoming aware that she had no idea of his identity. Her instinct was to confront him but she had no weapon and did not know whether this intruder was armed. If she had to call for help then her own presence there would be questioned. As she dithered, the back door to Amice's house opened and the little maid emerged to hang washing on the bushes outside. Quick as a flash the man opened the stall and went smoothly down the path towards the girl. Some seemingly amicable conversation ensued, the tall stranger nodding his head as if in agreement, and then simply walking on his way, unheeding. Dionisia seethed with fury, - she had not been able to hear the conversation but the girl had not been alarmed and the stranger had appeared satisfied with the encounter. Dionisia waited until the maid returned to the house and then retreated down the lane, her efforts fruitless. She would have to rely on those pesky twins.

Meanwhile the pesky twins, as Dionisia termed them, had discovered an alternative source of income. As they scuffed their ill shod feet outside the Abbey yard they were approached cautiously by a dark haired stranger with a request which gave them some amusement.....and possibly a way of earning money from two sources at once.

The man, who gave his name as John of Mottisfont, was interested in the child from the Abbey who was schooled by Master Copeland. At first the pair did not understand until it suddenly dawned on them that this must be the same child Dionisia had asked them to watch. Glee crept into their very being! They guessed which way Dionisia was heading....a child from the Abbey indeed.....it meant they could do but one search and receive money from two sources. What an admirable chance! John of Mottisfont told them that he had reliable information that the child had been removed to a small school in Milborne Port, but until he was sure this was true, he would not go there himself. All the boys had to do was to go there and verify his information.

Willing now they had an opportunity to double their income from just one task, the twins set out the next day for Milborne Port early in the morning, a good pace to start with but as the day grew warmer, their steps slowed.

As they approached the turning to Oborne, three horses swung onto the track from a fine house by the trackway. They were heading in the same direction as the twins, and for a brief moment, Daniel glimpsed Arnet, mounted in front of the leading man who called to the two others as they trotted to catch up with them.

"Noah! It's the child Dionisia asked us to watch! Let's follow! We can at least claim some coin from her if we can tell her where the child is!"

The riding party were trotting at a pace which made it hard for the twins to keep them in sight, but they quickened their steps, losing them at the top of the rise where the deer forest began. Dispiritedly they sat down by the side of the track, slashing at the undergrowth with sticks and looking around at this stopping place.

The boys sat silently for a while letting the sweat cool on their unwashed bodies, dreaming. The sound of a galloping horse interrupted their dreaming. The lone horseman was returning without the two other mounts, and minus the child mounted in front of him. The boys watched him pass them, nodding to him without a word. When he had passed, Noah identified him as the barber surgeon who often worked in Sherborne.

"I've seen him work in Sherborne sometimes...I'm sure it was he. Now what could he be doing with the child, and where did he take him?"

"The other two were young.....they have been left somewhere too."

"The school?" Noah queried, doubtfully.

Daniel clapped his hands in realisation,

"Yes! The school in Milborne Port.... It must be the same one the man told us to visit and watch for the brat. It's a little further on. Some years ago we joined a search for a boy who had been abducted from the school.....we must have been about fifteen summers old.....everyone was called out by that old fart the Coroner...it was his grandson."

Eagerly the twins resumed their walk, this time with a sense of purpose. Reach the school.....spy out the land..... let Dionisia know.....claim their coin....meet with John of Mottisfont again and deliver the news to him also – two lots of payment! Excellent!

Matthias didn't see Finn slip away to speak to two young men who were lounging by the gate of his schoolhouse. It was midday, a time when the scholars had a welcome break and Matthias saw no need to watch them as they converged in little groups, chatting, playing, relaxing.

He did notice, however, that Finn seemed very distracted when school resumed for the afternoon. His attention wandered, he was restless and was unable to answer simple questions. At the finish of the session Matthias asked him quietly to remain behind.

"Something troubling you, Finn?"

The boy shifted uneasily from foot to foot.

"I'm not sure, Master."

"You have some very strong opinions on certain matters, Finn...anything to do with that?"

Finn sighed. He knew Matthias did not entirely agree with his opinions, but he also knew that part of his education taught him that it was good to discuss and talk about differences.

"My half brothers were here today."

Matthias was taken aback. He didn't know the miller had any other sons.

"Your half brothers? I didn't realise you had brothers, Finn. Why is that troubling you?"

"My half brothers are from my mother's family. I haven't seen them for about three years, but they are still my brothers. They are seeking information. They asked me to help them. It is some work they have been asked to do."

"Tell me about this, Finn."

"My mother was married to a man who was hanged... .I'm not sure that he was my true father ...but he was the father of my half brothers."

Finn paused. He was uncertain how much he should reveal to Master Barton.

"Was he unkind to you, Finn?"

"He was an evil man who beat my mother in front of us. Afterwards she went back to her own parents hoping for help and took us with her, but she was tired and ill and they had no time for her."

"So Miller Felstead is not your natural father, Finn?"

Finn faltered, - he knew the miller had passed him off as his son to Matthias. Did that matter? He thought not – it was probably family pride.

"I watched her grow sicker and sicker until she died. When my mother died we stayed with her parents, but my half brothers led them such a dance that we were taken away by her brother who you know as Miller Felstead. I learned to respect him and called him father...I was quite young but the twins were wild and disobedient. They never called him father, they gave him no respect... they tormented me with dreadful stories of my mother and their father and were so disobedient that we were all relieved when they ran away and never returned."

Matthias listened in silence, understanding why Finn had been brought to education so late.

Finn paused for breath, hardly daring to believe that he had told his schoolmaster these shameful facts, wondering what Matthias would say to his father.

"So what has changed, Finn? Are you wanting to help them?"

"I'm not sure....they were so hateful to us, yet now they have no work, no coin....how could it be right that I would refuse to help them?"

"Where did you see them Finn?"

"They were outside the gate when we were released at midday. They recognized me and called me over."

Matthias felt a grave misgiving in this. He did not disbelieve Finn, - the lad had told the story willingly for the meeting had clearly disturbed him.

"What do they want you to do, Finn...are they asking you to speak to your father?"

"No, that's the strangest part. They want me to - " Finn hesitated. He recalled the twins wheedling tone, suggesting that they could all earn coin from an old crone in Sherborne by helping her to find the boy who had come to the school with the barber surgeon today. Finn was disturbed by this. He was not a dishonest boy; he had strong opinions concerning the coming split in the affairs of the king as he heard it from street gossip, - very strong for one so young - but he felt unease at the method of helping his brothers. He would much rather have begged his father or even Master Barton, to find them some simple work, or a dry place to sleep.

"Continue, Finn. You've said so much – finish the tale."

"They want me to tell them as many details as I can about Arnet, which they say will earn them money. That seems odd to me. I don't want to bring harm to Arnet."

"I think for the moment you should distance yourself from these brothers – Arnet is happy here and when the time is right he will return to Sherborne. What is the name of your half brothers?"

"Noah and Daniel Jolif, sir. Please don't think badly of me."

"I'm impressed that you have taken a sensible course, Finn."

Matthias sent a messenger to the Coroner after Finn had returned to his home. He didn't like the sound of this new development at all. Why would the Jolif brothers want details of Arnet's whereabouts? These boys sounded like the two the Coroner had been watching out for.

CHAPTER SEVEN

Divided loyalties emerge

———————— ❧ ————————

Sir Tobias was much amused as he watched the Abbot's angry face.

"I demand that the culprits are sought and made an example of... to impose a fine on the Abbey is preposterous..."

"Nothing more than the law demands," the Coroner observed coolly, halting the Abbot's tirade.

"What progress have you made on my other pressing matter?" The Abbot was himself much stressed by events at present, and the more personal matter of the child Arnet was troubling him.

"I have a good lead, due to some information received from Master Barton, schoolmaster at Milborne Port."

"Your kin, I believe?"

"Indeed, but that has nothing to do with the information, which has given me a line of investigation. As soon as I have some more definite news I will come back to you. Meanwhile, the matter of your fish pond still is ongoing, but you must also lay some blame on your own staff. You cannot be unaware of the local unrest fomenting daily. With that in mind surely the demesne of the Abbey should be more closely cared for?"

The Abbot's smouldering eyes were enough for Sir Tobias to know that the Abbot did not agree. However, he continued his journey down Cheap Street where he hoped to find the Jolif twins.

He was disappointed in this; there was no sighting of them in the general hustle and bustle of sellers and buyers in the market place.

Meanwhile, the boys were crouched lazily outside Dionisia's place, taunting her with news of Arnet's location. She was puzzled by the news....what possible connection could there be between Arnet and a small school in Milborne Port. It was too great a distance from Sherborne for Dionisia herself to walk. She would have to rely on these pesky boys. The prize was too great to abandon now.

The twins were unwilling to make the long walk again to meet up with their brother Finn, who had been reluctant to divulge any information, declaring that he knew nothing about the boy, and disappearing inside the school before they had time to dig deeper. They hadn't set eyes on Finn for several years and counted it a real bonus to have found him, so in their own time they would wander in the direction of the mill to waylay Finn. They would use him as a tool....he was young enough to be moulded to their way of life...what a chance!

They had underestimated Finn, and had reckoned without Matthias Barton!

Matthias met with Sir Tobias as soon as it was expedient for him to do so with the disturbing news of Finn's revealing conversation. Sir Tobias was very frank with Matthias, throwing caution to the wind.

"The general unhappiness in Sherborne is in part caused by the Abbot, as we know...the saga of the font is not over yet, and he is very jealous of the progress of the Alms-house, but the remainder of the unrest is a symptom of the failing state of the country. I hear dissatisfaction and mischief spreading from the counties in the South East... men are not afraid to kick the traces and exhibit their lack of faith in their superiors. We see it daily.....little acts of civil disobedience....a general disdain for the force of the law.....a feeling that there is something greater coming to distress us all."

Matthias was thoughtful. The Coroner spoke the truth, - it was known generally that His Grace the king was still influenced greatly by his lords who often fought for power amongst themselves.

"If trouble came, would you fight for the king?" Matthias hardly dared speak the word.

"I am the King's Coroner. I am the King's man through and through,"

"As am I," Matthias said softly.

"Pray to God it doesn't come to that," Sir Tobias replied. "But our local unrest is concerning me just as much. I have the Jolif twins and their rabble of young idiots, always willing to bring discord and strife, and now I learn that they have infiltrated to the place where Arnet was removed for safety. They have a disregard for law and so far have managed to escape my hands by taking their escapades right up to the wire - they will overstep it one day, but they display a cunning ability to evade justice. Now they seem to have joined forces with the busybody Dionisia from Acre Street - she who I believe may have hounded the Abbot and watched young Arnet. That causes me more troubled sleep than the twins; where has she got her information from - mis-information, I should say. She has a finger in many pies, none of them fragrant. Your young lad Finn needs watching

- you say he seems to have little regard for the King - a rebel in the making for all his concern for Arnet. And the pig incident - I'm as certain as I can be that this is the work of the Jolifs, but the fish pond, - now that's another matter. I doubt they have the brain power to organize that...their main target is the laws of the town and how to make as much mischief as possible, but the fish pond and the sheep rustlings and killings are a direct hit at the Abbot and Bishop Ayscough."

"He's a hard man so I've heard, the confessor to the King and hardly ever in his see...but at present residing in Sherborne Castle for a few days," Matthias observed.

"He appears to have little care for his tenants as long as the rent is forthcoming. Little sympathy was offered to the reeve Edmund. A proud man...a pity we have two such to deal with when we seem so beset with vexations."

"Let me deal with Finn and the mystery of the Abbot's tormentor," Matthias offered.

"I perhaps need to go back to the beginning and call on the reeve Edmund. I intended to do that immediately after that incident but other things took place. There was mention of a cloak which I neglected to follow. It is time I did so."

Sir Tobias knew it was time to look at the pattern of unrest in the town and deal with these restless factions before they got out of hand.

He accepted Matthias' offer of help gladly, relieved to have his assistance once more.

Dionisia set her mind to the battle she intended to have with the Abbot leading to a healthy income for herself and the satisfaction of hurting others who appeared more fortunate than herself. She felt things were not going as well as she had hoped. The twins were slow to act for her, and she was concerned regarding the unknown man she had observed at the house of Amice. It was no-one she recognized, and Dionysia made it her business to know the faces of most Sherborne folk. He appeared to be no threat to the household, for the little maid had made no gesture of fear; the conversation had been brief, and the fellow had made off, obviously satisfied with his answer. She wished she had been closer, could have overheard the conversation. She prided herself that she was good at listening in where she wasn't wanted.

She chuckled to herself as she remembered the flooded street; whoever had perfected that nuisance was very clever, but she knew it could not have been the Jolifs. They were too idle for a thing that clearly took much planning and physical effort.

Her morning plans took her in the direction of the Abbey where she hoped to see her friend who worked in the kitchens, inject her with more stories.....the strange visitor to Amice might serve her well for a tale of mischief.

The Abbey was still spoiled by rough scaffolding in places, work on the reconstruction slow, the font in All Hallows still not replaced much to the distress of the local townsfolk; much resentment still smouldered. Dionisia jostled for a position at the door where the spoiled bread would be handed out to the beggars of the town. She had no need of bread herself but she could not miss an opportunity for spreading word of what she considered to be the iniquity of the Abbot. She spotted a head rising above the women at the front of the small crowd; she recognized the back view of the stranger who she had watched at the home of Amice.

Now! What could he be doing here? What mission was he on? Dionisia edged forward, straining her well practised ears as the bread baskets were distributed suddenly by two young novices. She kept her eyes on the back of her quarry, pushing hard to get closer. He was within speaking distance of them but she noticed that he took no bread. Something appeared to pass between one of the novices and the stranger....a scroll of some kind....and before she had time to move closer, he had ducked out of sight and gone. Well! She sighed with satisfaction. Something was going on here....she would make it her business to discover exactly what!

Matthias rode down to Sherborne following his conversation with Sir Tobias. His scholars did not attend on Saturdays so he had the time to seek out the whereabouts of the woman Dionisia, who was unknown to him, and also to call on Mistress Amice to assure her that all was well with Arnet.

Although he had agreed to take this slight burden from the Coroner's shoulders, he was always mindful of the fact that he was not a Sherborne man, despite now being known by many and having made one or two friends in the vicinity. He first sought to discover whether the players were in town, for he had not seen Merrik, a player friend, for some time. Merrik had befriended the sister of the local barber surgeon, Ezekiel Jacobson although she still resided in Shaftesbury, some eighteen miles distant. Merrik and his players moved around from place to place with their great cart and Matthias always welcome the opportunity to chat with the genial actor. He found him enjoying the sun, his back to the wall of the enclosing Abbey garden. Merrik had developed a great respect for the peace and solitude of the Abbey and could often be found close by that great place.

Matthias settled himself down beside him, allowing the peace to drift over them both.

"What brings you into Sherborne, Matthias? I warrant it was not to talk to me!"

"No, although I'm always glad of the chance to catch up with your view on local events, Merrik."

"Ah. That sounds as though you might be searching for information."

"Indeed I am, but I'm not sure you can help in this instance." Matthias paused; he was unsure how much to tell Merrik. The actor was by no means a gossip but he, Matthias, had understood the conversation between himself and the Coroner was of a confidential nature, or at least some of it.

"Do you know of a local gossipmonger, Dionisia?"

Merrik laughed. He had studied Dionisia and her cohort of gossipmongers for their gestures, their twisted facial expressions and just for the fun of being able to imitate.

"Indeed I do, Matthias. What's your interest?"

"I'm unsure as yet. There's something unsavoury going on which involves a child I have been asked to protect. I just need to be able to identify her to start with...I don't even know what she looks like, although I suspect any townsperson would be able to direct me if she is as big a gossip and troublemaker as I've heard."

"Come with me.....I can probably show her to you!"

Merrik eased his frame from his comfortable position by the wall and hauled Matthias unceremoniously up to stand with him.

The two men set off through the Shambles towards the centre of the town, where Merrik was able to find Dionisia with little difficulty. Matthias watched her for a while, trying to imprint her features on his memory.

He pondered as he left Merrik on how he should proceed. He now knew what Dionysia looked like, would be able to identify her in a crowd and could watch for her. What could such a crone want with the child? He strode through town towards Mistress Amice's abode where he found her in her neat garden teaching her little girl some simple stitches, the tiny maid hanging on to her every word, watching the lesson enviously.

Matthias introduced himself and Mistress Amice eagerly asked him about Arnet's progress, happiness and health, her daughter listening to news of her brother earnestly.

The little maid ventured closer with a puzzled expression on her face. Matthias looked enquiringly at Mistress Amice, wondering what had confused the young serving girl.

She haltingly told them of the other visitor who had come, declaring himself to be Arnet's one time schoolmaster, and asking whether the child had been with the family for six years. She was unable to answer him properly, only having been with Mistress Amice for a year, and had been too shy to ask Mistress Amice whether Arnet was perhaps not their natural child. He had not seemed unpleasant, and thanked her for the information.

"What information did you give him, Senna?" Mistress Amice enquired, her hands unsteady as she sought her daughter's hand.

"Nothing much, ma'am....I could only say that he is schooled at Master Copeland's school usually but for now he has gone to a different school. I don't know why."

Matthias took Mistress Amice to one side, indicating that Senna was to take the little daughter indoors so that he could talk freely to Mistress Amice.

"I come from the Coroner, who is my father-in-law, and I have his blessing to discover what mischief is planned here.

You might know that my step- son is a pupil of Master Copeland, and that some six years ago he was abducted by a smuggling gang, causing both him and my lady wife huge distress which had a devastating effect on all of us. Arnet is now my pupil for a while to afford him some protection for I would not under any circumstances wish that experience on any other child."

Mistress Amice wound her fingers together as he spoke, but her eyes were calm, her posture resolute.

"If I speak the truth, may I be assured it will not harm my daughter or my family in any way?"

Matthias gave the assurance that she needed, and they walked a short way into her well-tended garden into the shade of a gnarled pear tree, blossom now shed.

"Arnet was brought to me by Dame Goffe .....he was possibly about two days old, and had been born of a local girl who had been seduced by one of the monks at the Abbey. Her angry family discovered this and left the baby with Father Abbot. I do not know who the family are, and I do not wish to. I have never enquired. It is nothing to me." Her voice was steady and Matthias believed her. This woman had no desire to draw attention to herself and her happy family life.

"I have always received financial support for caring for him, but I loved him as my own son....he came to me when my husband and I had given up hope of ever having a son or daughter to call our own. I have kept myself to myself....no neighbour could ever have seen our despair at our failure to conceive, and no neighbour was present to watch our love for Arnet grow and grow."

She paused to consider her next thought. Matthias let the silence sit easy as she met his eyes without fear. He considered her a remarkable woman with a strength of love and understanding.

"Recently I had a visit from a local gossip - Dionisia. I have witnessed her spite and gossipmongering, but I speak as I find, and until she called on me I had no reason to understand her malevolence. She wanted to alienate me from my son, wanted to undermine my belief in Arnet's parentage. She spoke in spiteful tones and demanded entry which I denied to her. I have earned my contented family, and I will not listen to her spite. I did not know of the stranger of whom Senna speaks, but I will not divulge details of Arnet's life to any stranger, whoever he may be."

"You speak well, Mistress Amice. I find it hard to betray a confidence but perhaps you will understand better if I indicate to you that a most high personage in the Abbey has found himself accused of parentage when parentage there is none. I do not mention his name, and you will undoubtably forget that we have had this conversation. This person is most anxious to discover the source of these unfounded rumours before they do irreparable damage to the very fabric of his domain. I see that it would appear that the woman Dionisia has gleaned sufficient information to put her entirely in the wrong direction but the appearance of another stranger rather muddies the path to putting an end to the gossip. You are doing well. Keep your husband informed so you remain a united couple against this slanderous attack."

Matthias took his leave soberly, determined now to discover the identity of the stranger who was also adding to the swirling pot - the lid of which must needs to be secured.

Amelisia was gathering fresh herbs on the fringes of the town, hoping to resume her favourite selling place at the bottom of Cheap Street. Her bruises had healed, her ankle was no longer swollen, her split lip had healed, she knew she must test her confidence and venture into the town with her little nosegays or she would lose her place, if indeed she had not already lost it. She had no selling tray now, and treasured the broken pieces for they reminded her of safer, easier times when her husband had been alive. Life was hard for one who believed in obeying the rules and minding her own business.

So on this day she fashioned a rough stick on which to tie her bunches of sweet herbs and took her place at the bottom of Cheap Street.

She had not been in her selling place for close on a month now, since the pig incident. She had felt too shaken and the swelling on her ankle took a time to subside, but now she knew she must try – or go hungry.

The market place was busy, she was reassured to hear the usual street cries, smell the familiar aromas and receive one or two nods of recognition from other street vendors.

When the door of Master Copeland's school opened to allow the scholars to tumble onto the street for a well-earned break, Amelisia looked for the young boy who had helped her with the tray and coins after she had taken a fall from the rush of pigs. She was painfully aware that she had brushed off their offer of help and had not thanked them adequately...they could so easily have ignored her and taken the coin for themselves. She remembered that there were two, although one of them had been more concerned than the other, who she recalled had seemed too embarrassed to come forward in the same way the other had.

Taking a penny from a customer, she almost missed him as he came slowly out onto the street, blinking in the bright sunshine and stretching his young limbs before turning to his friend who pushed past him to find the bun seller further up the street.

Luke smiled at Titus' eagerness and leaned against the warm wall of the school house, glad of the opportunity for a moment of sun. Amelisia approached him cautiously, not sure whether he would remember her, but she had reckoned without Luke's quick memory.

"Mistress! I'm pleased to see you have recovered – wait – I have something for you. Oh, I'm so pleased you have come out again."

He ran back into the school, bringing back with him the little tray he had made for her the last time he'd been at home. He had persuaded Martin Cooper to help him fashion it. It was smaller than her original tray, for he'd had to remember that it had to be transported back to Sherborne when he returned.

Amelisia trembled with emotion. No-one had ever helped her like this since her husband had died. She reached out towards Luke, and then shrank back, fearful of being taken for a beggar.

"I cannot, young master," she faltered, "I cannot pay you coin for this….it is indeed a kindness…but I must not accept it." She looked fearfully round to see if anybody was observing her.

"It is a gift. I made it for you myself," insisted Luke, anxious that he had offended her.

Amelisia's eyes filled with grateful tears; When was the last time anyone had offered her a gift? she took the tray from Luke, untying the little nosegays from her stick and arranging them with care in the tray. Luke had strung the tray with thin cord, enough to fit round her neck and balance at her waist.

"I thank you, young master." She pressed a sweet-smelling lavender and heartsease sprig tied carefully with long grass stems into his hand and Luke ran back into his schoolroom with a light heart and a fragrant gift.

Amelisia took up her place with a new confidence, unaware of Matthias who strode round the corner after Luke had disappeared. He stopped short in front of her, peered closely at her and startled her with his icy stare.

"A new disguise? I have my eye on you. Don't think you can continue this farrago of nonsense with the child by scrubbing the dirt from your face and hair and changing your clothes. He is not here. This trouble must end, mistress. The Coroner has you in his sights now."

Amelisia's trembling began again. She must have been seen taking the tray from the boy – she was marked down as a beggar – she would lose her pitch. Pleasure in her new tray vanished. With shaking legs she tore the cord from her, catching her hair in the rope in her haste. What to do? How to return it to the boy? She threw it down outside the door of the school and hobbled away, leaving her nosegays and fresh herbs to wither in the sun. Matthias watched her leave, satisfied that he had warned the troublesome woman. She had certainly cleaned herself up to continue her search for Arnet. She was nothing like as dirty and dishevelled as when Merrik had pointed her out to him.

Later, Luke found the tray, sadly rescued the herbs and pieced together the damaged edge of the tray where it had been tossed against the door.

"I didn't think she would do that," he said to Titus, as they retrieved the tray together.

"Something frightened her maybe," Titus surmised.

"She seemed so delighted once she knew it was a gift," Luke murmured. He didn't understand it; he needed to think and observe. Who or what had frightened her?

There had been another visitor that morning. He sat on the wall of the alms-house watching the building work, then walking through the Shambles to watch the school, back to the Abbey, on to the Abbey green....restless in his quest, unknown to everyone as yet. He only sought information – nothing more, but it had become an obsession with him and he must have answers.

Chapter Eight

More civil disobedience

It was time for a little more civil disobedience, John Coker decided. The emptying of the fish pond had been a huge success, despite the flooding of one or two streets in the lower part of the town, but thanks to the warm Summer, these were now dry. How had Dionisia, wretched hag, managed to bribe him into gossip and tattle for her silence about the sheep killings. He groaned aloud. He was certain she would ask more of him yet. They would have to be careful.

He met with his fellow conspirators to plan the next jaunt, all intent on causing irritation and nothing more to the Abbot and Bishop Ayscough for their stringent rule, and in the Bishop's case, uncaring and unsympathetic policies. Many good people in Sherborne paid rent to either the Bishop or the Abbot, the Bishop had not relieved the brewers of their croukpenny, the tax on ale, and the work demanded of many townspeople was hard, unrelenting with little pleasure from the arrogant Abbot, still insisting on regular payment towards the rebuilding of the Abbey.

Bishop Ayscough was in residence at the castle currently, having spent many months away from his see dealing with affairs of His Grace King Henry and his wife. He enjoyed his position as confessor to His Grace and was considerably puffed up with his own importance. Time to prick the bubble of self-importance with some harmless tomfoolery.

The men met in one of the many ale houses in Sherborne, careful not to use their usual place. In a dimly lit corner they planned their next move. The Abbot and the Bishop both had much to answer for in the eyes of the hard-pressed men of Sherborne, and although this group were active, there were few who did not support and applaud their efforts to draw attention to the hardships caused by arrogant, proud men. Humility was not one of the Bishop's attributes, nor, it has to be said, of the Abbot's.

"We need darkness for this affront," opined Henry Goffe, his eyes shining with excitement at the thought of this fresh plan. He was a strong, well-formed young man full of youthful energy and zeal. His aunt, Dame Margaret Goffe would not be impressed at his involvement, although she was no friend to the Abbot.

"Surprise is our best friend, and I do not expect us to have complete success at our first attempt, but it will send a message of discontent, which is our aim," agreed John Coker, as they split up outside the ale house to wend their way to their own homes.

They would wait carefully for a full moon, dry weather and the departure of the Bishop from Sherborne Castle.

Alice was truly mindful of the report she heard from Matthias regarding the child Arnet. It troubled her that he was for some reason the target of the gossip mongers, town underdogs - and through no fault of his family. As she carefully made copies on slates for her young scholars she pondered on the unfairness of life. She glanced through the door of the barn where she could watch the young ones as they congregated in happy clusters to chat before she called them in for their next session. The two girls were sitting together on the wall, heads together, watching the rough horseplay of Matthias' older scholars. She did not regret for an instant persuading Matthias to admit girls although there had been some dissension to begin with among one or two parents. They had weathered the criticism well. Now although the girls tended to keep themselves apart, it was working well. Her eyes sought out Arnet, anxious that he was not tempted to stray too far into the older boys' game for there was Finn. She did not distrust Finn but he certainly had leanings towards the rebellious faction, speaking enthusiastically about the unrest he heard from the East of the country. She knew he heard such things from traders who would have dealings with his father, the miller, and who travelled the whole of the South coast bringing news with them. Finn obviously listened, drinking in news of rebellions and minor uprisings.

She was aware that Matthias had shared the conversation he had with Sir Tobias and had also added the meeting Finn had with his two errant half brothers. It did not seem to have affected Finn, who was in school, as willing to learn as usual. Despite his interest in the doings of persons from neighbouring counties, Finn appeared compliant, showing little signs of wanting to explore the unrest further.

In fact, Finn was thinking a great deal about his two half brothers. He had told his father of the meeting, but the miller just snorted in disgust and hunched his shoulders, turning away from Finn.

"Have nothing to do with them, son. You have a greater chance of success than they. They are nothing but mindless trouble. Not a thought goes through their heads but how to make mischief - and it is not even sensible mischief. Now, if they were part of the town brigade of upstarts who pledge to make life as difficult for the Abbot and the Bishop as they do for the town I should be better pleased. Think no more of them – and watch over the young one they wanted to discover – their interest is nothing but mindless trouble."

Finn found it difficult to rid his mind of his father's response. He had not raised the matter again with the miller, working beside him in the lighter evenings, but he thought about it a great deal. He wondered whether his half brothers would know of this party of young men – his father had described them as upstarts but to Finn that meant young, strong opinionated men who were not afraid to act as they felt. He would not seek out his half brothers but if they appeared again, he might ask them what they knew.

The twins were meandering on their way towards Milborne Port. It was not a journey they enjoyed but it wasn't just Dionisia they served; the stranger called John of Mottisfont was also their most recent customer for information.

They had better hope of finding Finn again and worming some information out of him regarding the child in whom they were both so interested.

"What do you think Dionisia is up to?" Daniel asked his brother. Noah considered as he slashed at the undergrowth at the side of the track with a switch he had cut for himself.

"No idea. Something to make trouble as well as a bit of money for herself – otherwise she wouldn't be offering us pennies."

"Have you any coin today?"

"Enough for ale – let's stop at Oborne for a stoup - too hot to walk any further."

And by so doing the boys missed altogether the stranger walking briskly in the direction of Milborne Port, well advised of the whereabouts of Arnet by the maid of Mistress Amice, who had given more information than she realised.

Matthias was working with Davy, glad to expend some energy in the garden when the tall stranger approached him, openly, without guile.

Matthias drew him to one side and offered ale as they sat in the warmth of the afternoon sun. He studied the stranger; tall, dark haired, smooth face bland of expression, a well-made figure although slightly stooped in his shoulders. Nothing to dislike, Matthias felt, although the stranger seemed restless.

"How can I help you?" Matthias asked him.

"I am seeking employment," began the man, "I have studied in the halls of Oxford, I have experience in my previous life of educating boys in the disciplines....I would be grateful of the slightest amount of labour that you can offer me."

Matthias was taken by surprise. He had not mentioned at any time to any person the possibility of expanding his work force, in fact, he had not even considered it at all. He and Alice worked well together and although the school was flourishing, there was not room for a further expansion at present.

"My name is John Woke. I have travelled to this shire from neighbouring Hampshire; I need employment in order to remain here for a few months. Teaching is what I do best. I am informed that you have a young family and might be glad of a little respite from time to time in order to enjoy the pleasures of watching them grow."

Matthias was suspicious, wondering where the man calling himself John Woke had found this information. He and Alice were very satisfied with their current arrangements. Alice taught the younger children whilst Matthias himself enjoyed working with the older scholars, some of whom had challenging ideas and were proving astute and able under his patient, thorough tutelage. Davy and Elizabeth, Matthias' manservant and his wife, enjoyed the care they gave to Rose and Bettony, Luke being away with Master Copeland's school during most weeks. Matthias felt he would not be able to enjoy time away from the scholars, and he could not envisage a learned man nurturing the youngest pupils in the same way Alice did.

"I am flattered that you have been directed to me," Matthias told him, "but I have no plans to employ a third person. The school has not the space nor the finances to warrant it. I have to disappoint you."

The bland expression did not alter. If the man was dissembling then it was the answer he had expected, so for what reason had he come? Matthias was perplexed, suddenly remembering the unknown stranger who had called on Mistress Amice.

"I should think you would be more successful if you tried the Abbey in Sherborne," he suggested, watching the face for any sign of alarm or anxiety. "They run the school at the bottom of Cheap Street where my own son is educated. The good monks may have an opening for you there. "

It seemed to Matthias' shrewd eyes that this suggestion did not please John Woke. He sighed, finished his ale and gathered his limbs to rise from the wall on which they were sitting.

"Perhaps you are right. Tell me, do you have pupils who reside here with you?"

"No, all my scholars are by the day. They come in from the villages around. Most are sons of local merchants who see education as an opportunity to succeed in life."

"As indeed it is," agreed John Woke as he prepared to leave.

Matthias watched his retreating back as he left, swinging easily down the track towards Sherborne. Davy joined his master.

"Do you think he was a soldier?" suggested Davy, frowning as the figure receded into the distance.

Matthias decided another visit to Sherborne would be of benefit as soon as he could be free, and would attempt to see Luke, who was an observant youth. He might have noticed something of value from his position at the school.

"No, he did not have the bearing of a soldier.......soft, manicured hands, not those of a soldier. He was an educated man, but I wonder who gave him his information? Whoever it was, it was not correct."

"He clearly has no horse, either," remarked Davy. "That is quite a long walk if he is returning to Sherborne."

Matthias' feeling of unease continued but he was unable to account for it. The visitor had been pleasant, polite and open. Why did he feel uneasy about the encounter?

After a few moments, he directed Davy to follow him at a discreet distance on the nag.

Sir Tobias had determined to call on Edmund the reeve in an effort to retrace the course of the current tangle of misdeeds. He and William rode into Sherborne with this visit in mind.

They found Edmund at home, having spent the last few days in the fields overseeing the movement of flocks as the shearing was completed. The fleeces were now bound for packaging before being baled and transported to their ultimate destinations, initially by pack pony.

The Coroner took Edmund back over the events carefully, persuading him to recall shadows, details, feelings, sounds, smells. Edmund tried his best but the event was now a month behind them, details had all but faded from his mind. His son hovered nearby adding one or two details of finding his father unconscious, wounded, lying by the smouldering fire, bleeding heavily. Edmund felt obliged to answer the Coroner's questions but he was also very aware of the blanket of silence that some of his acquaintances had agreed should clothe these acts of irritation.

"Sir Coroner," the youth Tomas faltered, "there was one odd thing. When I returned with the bailiff, a cloak had been put over my father. We did not take much note of it at the time, the important thing was to take my father to a place of safety and summon a surgeon to stem the flow," the boy paused, seeing again the black cloak draped over the still form to attempt to retain warmth in the wounded man and feeling afresh his cold horror of believing his father dead.

"Someone must have approached......knowing the incident had occurred.....who?"

"The cloak was one item I had intended to pursue," Sir Tobias mused.

"What happened to the cloak?" William asked.

The boy indicated a hook on the back of the door, where Edmund's wife had hung the cloak and there it still hung, largely forgotten, although it was indeed a good, warm cloak of expensive wool. The Coroner noted it as an expensive cloak of excellent quality, abundant in fabric.

Sir Tobias left Edmund's dwelling with the cloak tidily folded over his saddle. It was a heavy garment, more suited to the monastic life, he thought, - a point which suddenly gave him cause for concern, and a further visit to the Abbot on the morrow.

Bishop Ayscough left the castle at the end of June to return to his duties in London. He did not greatly enjoy his stay in the place which was draughty, ill appointed in his opinion for a bishop, despite the riches of his own lavishly appointed apartments. He who had the King's spiritual care was pleased to be away from Sherborne.

He was not the only one delighted by his departure. John Coker assembled his fellow miscreants with excited plans for their next foray of disobedience. It was not their intention to be caught in this escapade, just to discover whether such a foray was possible – and to leave their mark in some way, to indicate their presence to the powers that be.

Sherborne Castle was built a little distance from the centre of the town, a small but stout castle, moated and with a small lakeside wharf. Situated on a hill not of very great height but high enough to give a commanding view of the surrounding countryside from the Great Tower, which could be seen for miles around. The South west gatehouse was the main point of entry over the wooden bridge which took visitors across the moat, but John Coker knew a different point of entry. The wharf was accessed by a flight of stone steps and so into the North gate, leading into the Barbican. Near there he knew was a small postern gate through which they could enter. He had a friend of similar rebellious leanings within the castle....it was always good to have an inside ear.

The garrison at the castle was maintained by a small cohort of soldiers who would be relaxed now Bishop Ayscough had left. There was a dungeon and prison facilities.... but the main task of the men on this foray was to leave evidence that they had succeeded in entering, leaving their mark to prove entry.

Sliding cautiously along the curtain wall, the men found the crumbling section of which they had been informed previously. It had reduced the height considerably, and John was able to haul himself up easily, keeping his profile crouched low lest there were guards, but there were none, there being little need now the Bishop had left and no prisoners to guard. Richard and Henry Goffe scrambled after him, weapons fast under their cloaks. Flushed with excitement, they kept to the perimeter of the inside of the wall until they reached the North East gate, manned by one sleepy guard inside his stone guard room. Silently they crawled on their bellies to the outside oven space, just the other side of the North Eastern gate. It was now dark, silent, the ovens doused for the night. They paused, listening intently for human sounds. Rustlings of roosting birds was the only sound. The occasional flare of a torch from the castle, a space of some two hundred feet from where they crouched could be seen, indicating the presence of either guests or the warden and his soldiers.

The kitchen was closest to them, nearer than the outer wall of the castle itself and John boldly stood up, indicating with his hand that the others should follow him. He found the door open, as he had arranged with his contact, and they were in! A young pot boy was asleep under the wooden table, rolled in a thin cloak; the three men bypassed him and silently advanced into the inner courtyard. The Great Hall was within their sight, but it was not what they had planned. They wanted the Bishop's personal rooms. Standing listening in the warm June night they understood that there were guests of the warden in the Hall; they would need to cross the Great Hall to reach the Bishop's personal rooms, so they settled under the grey stone of the castle to wait. They did not intend to leave without attempting to achieve leaving their mark.

They waited in silence for what seemed an age, hearing the rumble of voices from within the great hall, until suddenly the torches were extinguished and the space was empty....just waiting for them to cross to the Bishop's private quarters.

Their boots sounded too loud on the stone floor as they skirted the edge of the great room, the smell of the recently used torches lingering. Waiting tensely by the stone corridor leading to the suite of rooms used by the Bishop, the darkness and chill permeated their very being; they shuddered at the thought of being discovered here, but it was too late for such thoughts. There was no sound to disturb them; the Bishop had left; his suite of private rooms had been cleaned, the rooms were waiting only for the mischief that the three men had planned to execute.

One door only had been secretly unlocked for them, although the heavy wooden door was closed. John Coker knew it would yield to the press of the latch and indeed it did. It swung open for them, revealing the riches of the Bishop's inner sanctum.

Henry Goffe closed the door behind them for safety. There was a small glassed window looking out towards the green sward they had crossed on their way in to the kitchen and through this the moon gave enough light for Henry to grasp a candle from the aumbry, lighting it with his own tinder. The three gazed round the richly appointed room with awe. The magnificent wall hangings depicted the story of David and Jonothan, embroidered in heavy silks, vibrantly coloured. There was a fine woollen carpet covering the central part of the stone floor, upon which rested a throne-like chair cushioned in velvet, plush with purple cushions. The lingering indent in the cushions bore witness to the bishop's recent stay. The wine table to the side of the chair was delicately carved, highly polished, giving space for a chess set on top, the pieces carved from serpentine. Heavy leather tooled books sat on the shelf. There was a small fireplace set in the outer wall which had been cleared and now had a mounted tapestry in front of the empty grate. Hanging from the wall above the fireplace was the Bishop's own personal crucifix, gleaming with rubies picking out the figure of Christ, tortured no doubt by the splendour of the room.

The trio gazed in wonder at the magnificence of this inner sanctum for several moments, taking in the distant scent of the recently extinguished candles, perfumed oils, incense. They drew breath, exchanging uncertain glances. Now they were actually here they were suddenly uncertain how to proceed. They had planned to leave an unmistakable mark on the room, the message that the populace was able to stand against the power of the authority, especially when the authority appeared to confine them in the way the Sherborne folk felt ruled, used. The Bishop was not a familiar figure to any of the three – he came to the castle only when he needed to reside briefly in his see, preferring to spend most of his time at the court of the young king Henry. Their intended protest was at such riches as the vast sheep flocks, the rented dwellings, the ale tax, the disregard for the common folk of the burgh. Now they stood in this room, they couldn't quite bring themselves to use their daggers to slash at the rich hangings, score the wood of the delicate table, overturn the aumbry, with the smashing of the ornaments displayed there. They turned to each other; shame written in their eyes.

"We have to do something, at least," Henry Goffe whispered, uncertainly, moving ineffectively towards the larger table in the corner of the room, upon which were scrolls, quills, inks. The other two men followed him, aghast suddenly at the enormity of their actions.

Henry grasped the scrolls, threw them on the floor, unstoppered the inks and emptied them on the floor, staining the carpet and brushed the quills angrily with his hand, scattering them over the table in disarray.

"At least someone will know we've been here," he gasped, as they all turned towards the door through which they had come, soft on their feet, anxious to put distance between themselves and this small act of desecration. Their exit from the castle was surprisingly easy, shame on the guards, who should have been aware of the entrance of strangers, but were too relaxed after the bishop had left. The foray into the castle had brought them no great pleasure although they had expected it would do so.....but it certainly had given them information into the way to breach the castle in the future, should they so decide.

CHAPTER NINE

Finn runs into trouble

Davy returned to Barton Holding as the day faded into evening, stabled the faithful nag, fed her, retreated into the house hoping for a talk with Matthias and some supper. He had been successful in following the stranger who had sought employment with Matthias but was most puzzled concerning his whereabouts. The task had been most tedious, he explained to Matthias, because the stranger was on foot all the way, and although the nag was not the fastest steed, he had been obliged to keep well behind the retreating figure.

Some time on the way two young men appeared to join him, although it did not seem to Davy that they were very welcome company to the tall stranger. They had hung about him, keeping pace with him until they were within the centre of Sherborne itself, where Davy lost them, being unable to follow very closely at this stage. The stranger, however, had now behaved most oddly. He had hung around by the door of the guesten house, waiting with the beggars who had come to receive the broken breads from the monks' kitchen and table. Davy had tried to keep him in view, but of a sudden he was no longer there. Although he searched the diminishing crowds now the breads had been distributed, there seemed to be no trace of the man.

"Could he have gone into the Abbey?" Matthias wondered. He couldn't see how that could have happened but what other explanation could there be? He trusted Davy's ability to observe….so where and how had the man disappeared?

He pondered on this later as he and Alice prepared for bed. Alice was thankful that Matthias had not felt able to offer him work, for she sometimes wondered if Matthias was still truly satisfied with her ability to engage her charges now they had two young girls of their own. Bettony sometimes came into the schoolroom and sat listening to Alice as she worked, and once or twice Rose had escaped from Elizabeth and Lindy's capable hands and wandered in to see her. The boys loved the disruption which had caused a definite cessation of the work they were engaged on at that moment.

"Do you regret not offering him employment, Matthias?" she ventured, releasing her hair from its bone pins. Matthias caught a lock of her hair in his hands as he sat on the bed, easing himself out of his hose. He tugged at her hair playfully.

"What need have we of another teacher, Alice?"

"Hopefully none," she began. Matthias caught the slight hesitation in her tone. Was she trying to tell him that she would have been happy to have some release from the work? He would have been disappointed if she was tiring of the work, but perhaps she would not wish him to know. He loved working in partnership with her; perhaps he had been selfish, not noticing her own needs.

"I can try and find him once more if you would like me to, although his location seems a mystery. I cannot believe that he went into the Abbey….what cause would he have to do such a thing - he must have lodgings round behind the Abbey buildings."

Alice's heart sank a little. She had hoped for a reassurance that she was still good at her work. Matthias frowned; was he relying on Alice too much? She was still hardworking, well prepared but did he sense that she would welcome more time with their two little girls? Perhaps he should have explored the possibility of offering John Woke a couple of days work. Tomorrow he would seek out the man and revoke his previous refusal. That would gladden Alice's heart, he was sure. He turned to her as he swung his legs into bed, but she turned from him and although curled up into his body, there was no answering desire on this night. He put it from his mind, believing her to be tired from her dual role. There could certainly be work for this John Woke if he could be found, despite his unease.

The Jolif twins were delighted to have some news for Dionisia, hoping fervently that she would give them coin for this information. They hurried to her patch the following morning after their conversation with John of Mottisfont who they were pleased to have fallen in with on their way back to Sherborne, if indeed it could be called a conversation. He had been reluctant to talk to them but they had clung to him as he strode along, hoping to outpace them on his long legs, but they were insistent. They could not extract from him where he had been, although they guessed he had at least gone as far as Barton Holding to spy out the school.

Dionisia was mulling over her failed assault on the Abbot. She had the information which could damage him; she had her sights now on this stranger who for some reason was also interested in the child; she had Mistress Amice alarmed.....what else could she do to further her cause? She welcomed the twins in a half-hearted way — until they indicated that they had news for her — if she would pay for it. There ensued an argument about payment — Dionysia would not pay unless the information was of value. The boys would not divulge their pearls of wisdom unless they saw some coins. Eventually Dionisia fetched some coins from within her smoky inner room and laid them on the ground between herself and the boys, being careful to let them glimpse her dagger thrust through her worn belt. Her eyes glittered with malice at the very thought of being cheated by these saucy boys who thought they could feed her false information from her poor hoard of coin.

She was however more pleased with the information they gave her than she let them see, for this John of Mottisfont had told them that he knew without a shadow of doubt who the father of Arnet was. She questioned them eagerly about where she could find him......did he give any clues about how he knew? It was essential for Dionisia to find him and talk with him. She listened carefully as the boys gave her the best description of him that they could, greedily eying her little pile of coins.

The boys were not displeased with the coins she parted with, better delighted that Dionisia had told them that she was now seeking John of Mottisfont urgently and would pay more coin if they could find him, although she also intended to search herself. The twins left her to begin their search.

Matthias dispatched Davy to Sherborne the next day with instructions to locate John Woke and bring him back to Barton Holding where he would offer him employment. To this end, Davy was mounted on Matthias' own steed, the better to allow John Woke to ride pillion should Davy find him. He first began the search in and around the Abbey, where he was last seen. This yielded little, so he moved into the market place, busy as normal.

The Jolif boys had the better of Davy however. They had met John of Mottisfont as he was sliding out from the Abbey garden and by some cunning deception, persuaded him to walk with them to meet with Dionisia. They had not described the crone as dishevelled, dirty, an unwholesome specimen of humanity, rather they had described her as a person who could help him with his enquiries into the whereabouts of the child. They had not taken into consideration the well-cut clothes their quarry wore, crumpled from some kind of rough sleeping but no doubt fine woollen cloth, nor his well-modulated mode of speech. John of Mottisfont had no doubts regarding Dionisia, defining her immediately as involved in a piece of wicked mischief which in some way would damage the Abbot himself but more importantly, the child Arnet. He listened to Dionisia's request for information. She wanted to know who he was, where he was from, why he was interested in the Abbot's boy. His brow grew dark as he pressed his lips firmly together, his eyes never leaving the twisted figure clutched in Dionysia's fingers, her image of the Abbot, pierced in places by pins.

This was not for him. The boys watched him anxiously, poised to follow should he take flight. He was Dionisia's passport to riches….and theirs, too, to a certain extent. They had brought him here as requested - why would he now not speak with her? Whatever was going through his mind would most certainly not be divulged to this spiteful gossip. He kept his expression bland as he denied all knowledge of the boy, the Abbot, the town. He was, so he told her, a stranger visiting relatives in the area, ready now to leave for his home. He denied all interest in the child, claiming the twins were mistaken in their identification. He drew his woollen robe round his form as if to distance his whole being from her and strode away without a backward glance.

Noah snarled angrily, gripping his dagger in fury at the intransigence of this fellow. Raising his arm he flung the dagger after the retreating form. The force of his throw caught John of Mottisfont unaware; he stumbled, fell, grunted in surprise as his legs gave way beneath him, falling on his face into the mud, Noah's dagger embedded in the small of his back. Bleeding from the wound, he lay still, stunned, injured.

"You fool!" his brother rasped, grasping the hilt of the dagger and pulling it out with little regard for the victim. "Run!" he shouted, tossing the weapon as far as he could over the back of Dionisia's place. Dionisia scurried up the hilly track trembling and still clutching her image of the Abbot. She knew where to go – her sister had a place further up the track. She would not be welcome there but she needed to prove herself innocent of this...it would not do to be found near the place. The boys had vanished, putting as much space as possible between themselves and this unlooked-for crime.

Dionisia's hovel was not completely isolated; the cobbled narrow alley was used by those needing to connect with the market, so it was but a short time before the bleeding form of John of Mottisfont was stumbled upon by a passing trader seeking a short cut to the market.

Bailiff and market wardens carried the still form of this stranger into a more congenial place.

"Who is he?" the bailiff wondered aloud, troubled by the thought that this man, a stranger to this town, might die from this wound.

Davy came forward hesitantly. "I believe his name is John Woke," he volunteered, to the ring of faces surrounding the victim. "I was searching for him to bring him to my master, Master Barton of Milborne Port, who wished to offer him employment."

John Woke stirred, groaned, gasped with pain and the bailiff, galvanized into action, sent to the Abbey for a pallet on which to lay him to convey him to their apothecary brother who would treat him.

Later, heavily bandaged and distinctly sore, John Woke sat cautiously upright behind Davy on Matthias' good mare, every jolt making him wince. The monks had cleansed and dressed his wound which fortunately had been deflected by his thick robe, causing a nasty wound but not a fatal one, nor even one which would have required stitching. Having identified him as one to whom his master intended to offer work, the bailiff had decreed that Davy should take responsibility for this man.

Matthias was pleased to observe Davy riding back towards Barton Holding with a pillion passenger, less pleased when he learned that the man had been injured in an attack and that Davy had been told to be responsible for him.

Alice was put out by Matthias' feeling of annoyance at how the incident had developed and insisted that John Woke should be treated as a guest for a day or two until his injuries allowed him to continue his life in whatever way he chose.

She was careful not to give any impression that he might well be usurping her position in the school room. Her inherent breeding made her instantly a good hostess towards a stranger, injured and presumably far away from home. Matthias for once found it impossible to read her face. Normally he had only to look at his beloved wife to know what was going through her mind, so close had they become since Luke's abduction, which had taught both of them priceless truths about themselves as well as each other. This time she was inscrutable.

John Woke was a good guest, no trouble. He was quiet, refined, polite and very grateful. He was not inclined to talk about his ordeal, apart from saying he had been trapped in an unknown ally whilst searching for the way to the Abbey, and set upon by two youths. He kept the true details to himself.

Whilst here, it afforded him the opportunity to look around, see the scholars, who would be in attendance on the morrow and possibly enquire discreetly concerning the child in whom he was so interested, - if indeed he was here. It appeared from conversation that Matthias only took boys from local families and above a certain age. He could bide his time.

Matthias had a strange compulsion to discover more about the attack on his guest. There was something about him that caused Matthias a frisson of alarm, although exactly what he couldn't say. Perhaps it was his unwillingness to revisit Sherborne with a view to discovering the identity of his attacker, more likely it was because the story about trying to find his way to the Abbey didn't add up – the runnels and tracks described by him were nowhere near the Abbey – and Davy had tracked him to the Abbey before, so he clearly knew in which direction the Abbey lay. But in conversation John Woke appeared to be precisely what he claimed – a traveller seeking relatives, having arrived a few days ago from neighbouring Hampshire; Matthias was no stranger to deceit, half truths and dissembling, having learned much of the shadier world of men since he first met the Coroner, and was on his guard to discover more about this man.

Alice had made her position clear to him – he must be treated as a guest with courtesy, not suspicion. She herself found no fault with him apart from the fact that he might be just about to take some of her work from her. Looking back on the original conversation with Matthias she knew she should have made herself clearer, but what was done was done. She allowed herself to talk with him about the work she did and found him interested in her method with the younger pupils and well informed concerning the disciplines of the older pupils. After a while he brought the subject round in a very subtle fashion to how many pupils, from where and of what age.

Matthias frowned, catching Alice's eye from his seat across the table. She read caution in his glance, and confined herself to just talking about numbers before calling for Elizabeth to clear the table.

John Woke professed fatigue and retired to the small chamber shown to him previously. He was not dissatisfied with his information – tomorrow perhaps he would see the child. He eased himself onto the small bed, wincing at the smarting from his wound. What did that dreadful woman want of this child? What mischief was in her mind? Perhaps he should speak privately with Matthias – but there was so much at stake for him – he hardly knew whether he dared. He slept uneasily

The discovery of the open doors at the castle had caused concern. The rich carpets were stained, papers had been scattered around and the cleansing and tidying was of some concern before the Bishop's next intended visit. It was obvious that there had been intruders, but strangely there did not appear anything missing, just disturbed and stained. The captain of the castle guard could not account for the happening and was little inclined to discipline those who had been on duty that evening, feeling that little harm was done. The bishop had left, there were few guests at present, certainly no-one of any importance, and no prisoners in the cells either. The incident was dismissed as unfortunate, without so much as a mention to anyone in authority. However, the ease with which they had been able to enter was stored in the minds of the intruders and would be used in the future with disastrous effects.

Finn was fired with zeal for fighting the injustices of his world as he saw things. He had heard his father mention the young hotheads of the town who were intent on causing the Abbot and the Bishop as much inconvenience as possible, and he was keen to find them. Wasn't he now thirteen, soon to be a man, and very willing to play his part? He was wise enough to realise that his newly met half brothers were not going to be his way to find them, so he set about listening to the adult talk, offered to go into Sherborne with his father when he took the cart down for supplies. Once there he had no clear idea how to seek for them, nor even who they were.

His father had business in town so Finn had leave to browse the market place for a little time. He kept his ears and eyes open. There was no sign of his half brothers until he was nearly ready to re-join his pa. He felt he had wasted his time in coming into Sherborne - he had no idea where to find the young men he was seeking, nor how he could act with them - it all seemed beyond his grasp, which disappointed him. Emerging from Acreman Street he ran straight into Daniel, slithering along the cobbles furtively, clutching bread and a small pot of cheese. Daniel wasted no time – he gripped Finn's arm and dragged him with him, Finn protesting volubly that he was due to meet their father who would not be best pleased to be kept waiting.

"I need you to do something for your loving brothers," Daniel snarled. Finn had no choice but to allow himself to be dragged down the back alleys to where Noah was hiding. Daniel had a grip of iron and Finn's arm was sorely marked. Noah grabbed the bread from Daniel and tore at it frantically. Finn became nervous of these two – something was very wrong. Noah was dirty, pale faced, eyes ringed with shadows – the place was the furthest ruined house in a row of ex plague houses. It smelled foul, was dark, the runnel leading to it was deserted, slimy and little-used.

"The man – John of Mottisfont – do you know him?" Noah rasped, hoarsely. Finn shook his head vehemently, denying all knowledge of such a man. Daniel punched him in the stomach, doubling his younger half-brother over painfully.

"I've only come into Sherborne this morning with Father - I don't know many people in Sherborne -I'm looking for the young men who irritate the Abbot," he gasped, when he could breathe again.

"Well, you can stop that nonsense and do some searching for us now," Daniel declared.

"They won't want you - Henry Goffe is too fine for the likes of a miller's bastard son," sneered Noah, swallowing his half-chewed mouthful of bread.

Finn took careful note of the name – at least he had a name to help him.

"We need to know what happened to the man called John of Mottisfont," Noah continued. "Is he still alive?"

"What have you done?" Finn gasped, horror-struck at being suddenly involved in their lives. The brothers exchanged wary glances.

"An accident - he was injured - we need to know whether he recovered."

"Which of you hurt him?" Finn gasped, edging away. Daniel was having none of it. He pushed Finn onto the ground and stood over him threateningly.

"We're family. Don't you dare run to father. Noah threw his knife - we can't move until we know what happened to him."

"What did you do with the knife?"

"Tossed it away," came the terse answer.

Finn scrambled to his feet. "I need to meet with Father now. I'll come back tomorrow when I've had a chance to ask, but there's no furore in the town - everything seems normal. The Bailiff isn't in evidence, searching. Maybe he recovered and returned to his people...."

Daniel scowled heavily, still gripping Finn hard but suddenly relented, unwillingly allowing him to leave after demanding that Finn should meet them the next day. There were distinctly unpleasant things Daniel would do to Finn if he did not appear – Finn had no doubt that Daniel was capable of keeping his word as he rubbed his sore arm and examined his stomach's tenderness.

He was silent as his father drove the cart home laden with items needed for the mill. The next day was a school day - he wondered how he was going to meet, how to discover the injured man - he knew his half brothers could be violent with no regard for law and order - and he would bribe them with more names for him to align himself with what his father called young hotheads. That at least would make the journey worthwhile, but he was now wary of Daniel's temper if he should not find the answers the twins were seeking. Why on earth was he involved in this? He did not want it – he was happy at Master Barton's school. This could spoil all that.

It was easy for Finn to evade Barton Holding the next day; he walked from the village as usual but instead of branching off towards the school-house, he kept on the main track and soon was able to cadge a ride in the cart of a pedlar travelling with his wares to market. It was still early in the day so he did not meet the Jacobsons on the road - they would have wondered why Finn was travelling away from school. When the pedlar put him down in Sherborne Finn was at a loss as to how he could discover the fate of the man wounded by Noah.

By a stroke of luck the Abbot's bailiff was in town, collecting rents from stall holders - much resented, bearing in mind the rent, yet again, had risen. Finn overheard one trader comment on the rise – too high – simply to pay for the repairs to the Abbey – what injustice. Greedy Abbot. Finn followed the bailiff carefully and heard other such comments. This injustice was precisely what made Finn anxious to make contact with the young men – but for now he had another task. He waited until the Bailiff reached the last trader, and then softly tugged on his sleeve.

The bailiff turned to regard the youngster, nearly as tall as himself, clad in simple hose and doublet, under- shirt clean, open at the neck. His clear blue eyes were anxious, his voice was well modulated, articulate although as yet unbroken.

"Sir, there was a man wounded in town a few days ago – I think he might have been a neighbour of my father. Do you know what happened to his body?"

The bailiff regarded Finn silently, assessing his honesty.

"Enquire at the Abbey, young man. He was taken there." He turned away, anxious to complete his work with the market traders.

Finn trudged to the Abbey, dodging piles of detritus from the market place. He had not been here before on his own and hesitated before knocking on the door of the guesten house. It was opened by a lay person to whom Finn had to explain his mission.

The girl was a little older than Finn, well-scrubbed and garbed in simple tunic covered with a white apron, a serving girl, but she knew the answer to Finn's question without having to search for a more senior being.

"He went away with a serving man from Milborne Port once he had been well bandaged and cleaned, his injury was not great, stunned and sore, the aim was not powerful enough they said to do much damage. He left with a serving man who said his master was offering him work."

Finn was stunned. Milborne Port! Exactly where he had come from that morning....and just where he did not want his brothers to go again.....now what was he to do?

CHAPTER TEN

Idle dreams and careless talk

Matthias was surprised at the absence of Finn from his usual place but had no opportunity to chase after him on that particular morning. He glanced round the assembled scholars, waiting patiently for him to begin. He was pleased with the progress of the group, learning to think for themselves. The room was so unlike the beginning of his school – he had made great strides since the opening and was now recommended by local merchants who appreciated the education of their sons. The daughters? Some, he knew, were still looking askance at the inclusion of the few girls but he did not regret the decision. It had helped Ennis, his first girl pupil, included by Alice during his absence when searching for Luke so many years ago.

A simple logic exercise swung into a pleasing exchange of statements; Matthias was impressed by how well one or two of his scholars were now able to express their views and how informed some of them were becoming. After a short interval during which Matthias was delighted with the way their arguments were progressing, one, Simon Fishlake, paused in his rhetoric to mention the absence of Finn. Matthias had noticed a friendship between the two boys so felt it worthwhile to allow the pause.

"Did you not see him on his way to school this morning?"

"Finn always walks on his own.....so he leaves before those of us who come mounted."

"Who else walked alone this morning?" Silence met his question...most of these boys came mounted from a little distance. Finn lived with his father at the mill which was an easy walk to Barton Holding.

"He had prepared some arguments for this exercise," Simon volunteered, "he would not want to miss the opportunity to put forward his ideas."

"I will send to the mill to enquire after his well-being," Matthias decided, steering the boys further on in their debate.

He made sure that the group heard him ask Davy to ride out to the mill to check on Finn's health, and thought no more of it as he invited their guest into the school to see the work done.

John Woke showed a lively interest in the ongoing work, engaged with one or two of the boys and then asked if he might also see Alice at work. For some unfathomable reason Matthias was not keen for him to do so and made a simple excuse to avoid him seeing Alice at work.

"If I am able to offer you work when your wound is fully recovered it will be with my older pupils," Matthias told him. John Woke did not press the issue further; Matthias could not help but notice that he tried hard to peer round the curtained recess where Alice worked. He seemed disappointed when they moved on, out of the hearing of the younger boys.

John Woke retired to his room after his tour of the school for his wound, although far from fatal, was sore and he needed to rest. He was absent, therefore, when Davy returned with the disquieting news that Finn had indeed set out for school as usual that morning, but unaccountably had insisted on leaving earlier than normal. The miller was angry rather than concerned, Davy reported, for he did not want Finn to waste the chance of betterment he had been given.

Matthias and Alice discussed Finn's absence when they took their break. Alice was disappointed in him; Matthias was more thoughtful; he had heard some of Finn's thoughts on the political state of the country....verging on dangerous talk, as young boys tended to do. He sought Simon before they resumed afternoon lessons.

"He was becoming interested in finding the young men who are intent on plaguing the Abbot and the Bishop," Simon explained. "He talked about it greatly – said we should be the next generation to stand up for our rights – he may have gone to find them, but I don't know what might have brought this on...it was really just idle talk and possibly dreams."

"Idle dreams and careless talk may land you in trouble," Matthias cautioned him, "some who hear might declare it treacherous talk."

Simon appeared somewhat downcast at Matthias' warning, for he too was fired with the need to stand up for the rights of the ordinary people who had to fight to live. Nothing seemed fair to their young minds. At eleven, twelve, thirteen these were youngsters who were nearing adulthood....soon would be making their way in a world which surely would see change, and not all of it peaceful, Matthias was afraid.

He guessed Finn had gone to seek the rebellious young men in Sherborne; he dispatched Davy to try and find him before the lad found himself in trouble.

Brother Jonas was a worried man. He had watched carefully for John of Mottisfont for the last two days but he had not appeared. There was nobody he could confide in; he knew he had sinned in aiding the man but he had acted on a whim which he now regretted bitterly. The man had needed somewhere to sleep, he had lost his cloak and was in serious trouble himself. Now Brother Jonas was experiencing a crisis of conscience – what had befallen the unhappy man? Should he speak out – what on earth had possessed him to involve himself in the troubles of another - he knew the man from a previous meeting some years ago – what had possessed him to allow him entry to the Abbey precincts to shelter at night in the detritus of the building works. He had no fear of being discovered there for the lay builders left before dusk, and John of Mottisfont was very aware that he must not be discovered. Brother Jonas dithered in his predicament, scanning the small crowd of beggars who gathered to receive the mercy bread, but there was again no sign of John of Mottisfont.

Later he was sent to serve in the guesten hall where he anxiously surveyed every guest who came in but there was no sign of him. In any case he didn't think he would dare to enter into any part of the Abbey in broad daylight – there was too much at stake for him. Brother Jonas wished he could have answered the simple question which burned at John of Mottisfont's soul – but he was unable to do so.

"You are expecting someone today, Brother Jonas?" the cellarer monk asked him.

"No, no Brother Brendan....I have a little trouble with my eyes today – I need to peer very hard in order to see accurately."

Brother Brendan was sympathetic and suggested that Brother Jonas should pay a visit to the infirmary. Brother Jonas hastened off to obey, glad to be away from Brother Brendan's questions, for guilt was overcoming him.

Brother Francis in the infirmary produced an eye wash for Brother Jonas who meekly allowed the infirmarian to examine his eyes, feeling that he was wasting time, adding to his sin. He was about to leave to return to his duties in the guesten hall, when Brother Francis commented quietly that the injured man he had tended a few days ago had looked very like one of the brothers who was now elsewhere....hadn't Brother Jonas worked with him in the scriptorium for a while? Had Brother Jonas noticed him?

The world stood still for Brother Jonas for a minute. He was unable to meet Brother Francis' eyes as he mumbled a denial and fled. He found himself shaking as he leaned against a cool whitewashed wall in the corridor leading down to the guesten hall. An injured man? He hadn't known. How could John of Mottisfont allowed himself to be brought into the Abbey? How injured was he...and where was he now? He controlled the trembling in his limbs and deliberately measured his tread as he thrust his shaking hands into his sleeves to hide his weakness.

Back in the guesten hall Brother Brendan was occupied with some merchants who needed a night's accommodation, so he was spared further questioning, but he took advantage of the young serving girl while there was opportunity.

"Were you here when the injured man was brought here?"

She most certainly was. A local serving man claimed him – he said he was called John Woke, and his master wanted to offer him employment. The pair left by horseback to travel the short distance to Milborne Port.

Brother Jonas was perplexed. John Woke? Why would he give that name? Whatever was going on? He sought out the Prior with a heavy heart. Perhaps it was time for him to tell what he knew.

116

Dionisia was tired of living in her sister's poor house. It was crowded with her things, her stinking herbs hanging from the ceiling, pots of messy flower water on every surface. It was too clean for her liking and she had never seen eye to eye with her goody goody sister. She had heard no hue and cry for the man Noah had knifed, so it was time she returned home to act on the Abbot. If the boys would give her no further help she would have to be open and bold with the good Abbot.

Perhaps she should try to reach the school in Milborne Port herself and take the child with her to see his father, the Abbot. Dionisia was full of her own schemes, ignoring her age, her lack of ability to think further than one day at a time; she could not see the drawbacks of her own plan. She dreamed of riches, of reward for her snooping….the way forward was not something she considered with any common sense now she had gone so far in her great scheme. She hugged herself with glee as she hobbled through the narrow passage way to her own place.

She was not pleased to find Noah and Daniel ensconced in her murky room. Daniel had lit a fire near the entrance and was frying some fat bacon. The smell made Dionysia's mouth water despite her annoyance at their temerity. Thinking she would stay with her sister for some time, the boys had lost no time in moving their things into the place, leering at her unpleasantly. Noah folded his arms and regarded her with a scowl.

"So what's this great plan you have, eh?"

"I could go to the bailiff and turn you in," she began.

Daniel confronted her with elbows akimbo, feet planted sturdily apart, blocking the light from the door. The bacon fat sizzled in the cracked pot, grease from the pan dripping onto the hot ash.

"There's plenty we can tell him about you, you old hag. You plan to kidnap the child – what for? The woman isn't wealthy – the child is just a child of the street here in Sherborne – you can hang for that."

Dionisia made no reply, instead retreating further into the smoky depths of her home. She found herself trembling with fury. How dare these bully boys turn against her – she felt in her skirts for the effigy of the Abbot to hold tightly in her hand, and by doing so alarmed Noah, who watching her closely was suddenly certain that what she held in her hand was a weapon.

He leapt over the fire, disturbing the wood and flames as he did so, advancing on the woman with a snarl. Everything happened so quickly after that. Daniel lunged for Noah who had drawn his knife, Dionisia backed further into the hovel to escape the reach of Noah's knife, the bacon fat tipped onto the fire, igniting rubbish lying close to the pot of fat the boys had procured for cooking which flared into life faster than expected. Dionisia's howl of fear rang out at the same moment that Noah's knife sliced fiercely into her arm. She collapsed to the floor. Daniel grabbed a battered box which he used as a shovel to scoop up ashes and sparks from the fire which he flung at the fallen form of Dionysia. Noah dropped his stiletto, attempting to follow Daniel who was now in full flight. He stumbled as he reached the remnants of the still burning fire and fell onto the cracked, leaking pot in which the fat was now spitting with heat. Bellowing with pain he scrambled to his feet, burns on his legs, hose smoking, hands smarting with pain. Limping heavily, sobbing breath impeding speed, he limped after his brother, leaving Dionysia unable to escape the fire now smouldering into fierce life, fanned by draughts in the hovel. Fire was a fearful event in these narrow alleyways; Noah made good his faltering escape, unheeding of Dionysia, whose charred body was discovered much later.

Sir Tobias was summoned to the scene, for surely one of his chief duties as coroner was to investigate deaths. He picked his way over the smouldering remains of the humble dwelling, smoking still. Local helpers who had been alerted by smoke had doused the flames with water from the nearby stream carried in their leather buckets. Their quick actions had prevented the fire spreading to other dwellings, much to the obvious relief of the careworn faces which surrounded him as he looked round.

The pan used to fry the bacon was upturned near the source of the fire, blackened now with heat. Some evidence of spilt fat was visible. The body of Dionisia was beyond the fire, lying on her face. There was blood nearby. Sir Tobias bent and turned her over carefully. He could see the gash made by Noah's weapon scoring her upper arm, but she had clearly died by fire. Her clothes were charred, her hair was singed, the flesh on her hands and face were blistered unpleasantly. If it were not for the gash on her person, Sir Tobias would have assigned the case to accidental death, but the wound indicated beyond doubt that there had been another involved.

He straightened up, surveying the circle of silent neighbours clustered round.

"This is Dionisia?" Various voices muttered an agreement.

"She may have been trouble but she did not deserve to die like this," he heard an old man grumble.

"What sort of trouble?"

"She was a trouble maker, my Lord Coroner, you know that, but nothing serious – she just loved to stir us all up.

Sometimes it was unpleasant, but she never should have burned to death." The rheumy eyes of the old man were wet with tears of shock.

"Did anyone see who she was speaking to before she died? There was some attempt at wounding her which may have become more serious if it were not for the fire. How did the fire start?"

"She had fled a few days ago to stay with her sister – she returned today, but there had been some young men lodging in the place –" volunteered another neighbour, pushing her hair away from her face, wringing her roughened hands together in distress at the sight of the corpse.

"The brothers Jolif by any chance?"

The watching crowd would not meet his eyes; there was no reply; they all knew how dangerous the Jolif brothers could be if their tempers were roused.

The crowd began to drift away; the bailiff saw no reason to hold them; they had work to return to, had come to douse the flames and been detained at the Coroner's pleasure.

The old man with the rheumy eyes stayed.

"Two young men ran away."

Sir Tobias had to lean in close to understand him, lisping information through gummy wet lips.

"Why did she leave to stay with her sister – and how do we find her sister? I didn't know she had a sister."

But if the old man knew more, he would not say; he shuffled away. The bailiff was surprised her sister had not come before him, but he had old history with Dionysia who had appeared before him many times. The Jolif twins came into the Coroner's mind. The Jolifs and Dionisia would be a potent mix for trouble. Sir Tobias' eager nose twitched. It had to be them! But why?

Davy arrived in Sherborne as Sir Tobias was scouring the ruined hovel of Dionysia and arranging for her body to be removed to a better place. He hoped it would be simple to find Finn, but he was dismayed to catch sight of him talking in what seemed to be a very deferential fashion to a young man with dirt-streaked face, torn tunic, one hand on the handle of a knife thrust through his belt. He seemed to be entreating Finn to do something for him, certainly an element of desperation in his demeanour. He saw Finn shaking his head vigorously, noticed the tightly balled fists of the young man and stepped forward to intervene before Finn could come to harm.

Davy was surprised at how authorative he sounded as he accosted Finn with more confidence than he felt.

"Whatever errand you are on Finn, Master Barton would have you return to school immediately. My horse will take two of us. Come."

Finn glared at the young man who shrank away from Davy's gaze, and allowed himself to be led away, relieved at his unexpected rescue.

Once round the corner and out of sight of the man, Finn shook off the hand which Davy had placed on him.

"Am I in trouble? Will I lose my place? Can you give me more time in the town before we return?"

The conflicting emotions played across Finn's young face. He was anxious to make contact with the protestors whom he believed were doing the best they could to force the Abbot and the Bishop to play more justly with the townspeople, but also afeared of losing his standing with his father and schoolmaster...difficult emotions for one as young and untried as Finn.

Davy however stood firm.

"Finn, we need to return now. That young man meant you harm. You will be safer in school. Whatever you intended to discover here in Sherborne will be here for you to discover another day. If you linger, you may not live to see another day if you have crossed him."

Reluctantly Finn permitted Davy to lead him to where he had stabled his horse, and mounted clumsily behind him. Daniel watched them leave, uneasy, determined to revisit Finn. Noah's burns were festering and Daniel cursed Finn again and again for his refusal to help them. He did not dare seek help for Noah just yet, but as soon as night fell he would go to the witch woman for poultices. Daniel felt sure they were now in serious trouble but as long as they lay low, they would survive – as usual. Curse Finn! He hadn't finished with his young half-brother yet.

CHAPTER ELEVEN

Finn's return

Davy delivered Finn to Matthias as the scholars were preparing to leave for home, Matthias preparing to escort the boys using the nag normally used by Davy.

He dismounted at once as Finn scrambled from the horse and stood sullenly before him. Alice observed his posture...uncertain, trying hard to appear insolent, failing. She stepped forward.

"Matthias, let me give Finn some refreshment after his day out; I'm sure he is both hungry and thirsty, let alone shaken after the ride behind Davy. You can speak with him when you return."

In her eyes Matthias read the wisdom of calm discussion rather than angry confrontation with a lad who did not fully understand his own mind. He thanked God for the quiet wisdom of his wife. He remounted the nag and moved off to the waiting scholars, leaving Davy to unsaddle and rub down his own steed. Alice smiled at Finn who stood uncertainly now, bemused by this sudden turn of events.

"Come in to the kitchen, Finn. Elizabeth has baked today, and there is cool water for a parched throat. Tell me about your day. What made you miss school today?"

He sat on the bench by the window which overlooked Alice's herb garden. The bees were working the lavender;

123

the fragrant smell of Elizabeth's baking lingered. He watched Alice fill a cup of water for him and bring a fruit pastry from the batch waiting to be stored. It was a peace he had forgotten in the turmoil of his life. Finn was enjoying his studies although he found concentration hard; he was aware of his father's desire for him to be better able to run a business despite the somewhat fractured family circumstances – his sisters could not run the mill, and his father was already relying on him for calculations although there was no reason to believe his father was not successful still.

He suddenly realised how hungry he was, biting into the juicy pastry. The crisp shell of pastry was still slightly warm, the fruit sharp, full of flavour. He took a long drink of water and tried to think of a suitable answer to Mistress Alice's question. Finding none, he told the truth.

"I had to meet with my half brothers to give them news of a man they had injured...they were quite threatening...I didn't want them to come here again and cause trouble."

"Why would they cause trouble, Finn? What hold do they have over you?"

Alice refilled his cup of water, relieved to see that she did not have to force answers from the boy.

"Could this be something to do with Arnet?" Alice wondered, helping herself to a pastry absentmindedly. It was strangely companionable in the kitchen; Elizabeth was out, Davy was busy in the stables and Lindy had taken the children to paddle in the brook.

"It is, partly," Finn admitted. "My half brothers wanted information about Arnet. Not for themselves – for an old woman they hang around – she gives them coin for information."

"Have you given them any information?"

"No Mistress Barton. I would not do that, but they have also been involved in a wounding – they needed to know whether the man was dead or not."

"So they asked you to go into Sherborne and enquire on their behalf?"

"Yes – I thought if I did that it would keep them from coming here to see Arnet for themselves."

"Have they threatened you, Finn?"

Finn considered. They had, but truth to tell he was a little nervous of what they might do now they knew where he was. He was no coward, but he could see no future in picking a fight with the twins – known for their ruthless trouble making and vicious temper – he remembered the pain of the stomach punch.

"Not exactly, Mistress Barton….but I'm afeared of what they might take it into their heads to do if I don't give them some response – but I don't want to be involved with their life. It's not fair!" The last was a cry for help, Alice recognized, as the words were wrung from Finn.

"The worst bit was when I'd found someone to tell me what they wanted to know – they said the man was here in Milborne Port, so I had missed school for nothing – likely in trouble with Master Barton as well as my father."

Alice was startled; she thought of her guest – apparently keen to see into her little room to look at the younger boys, where Arnet was. Where was Arnet now she suddenly wondered. Had he already been collected by Ezekiel? Were Ezekiel's boys waiting with him? She rose hurriedly and opened the kitchen door the better to see outside to where the boys always waited for Ezekiel to meet them.

She breathed a sigh of relief when she saw the three of them waiting by the fence, but also with them, talking animatedly was John Woke. He had a hand on Arnet's shoulders.

Alice was no fool; no point in alarming the man. She took a step outside, calling to the party.

"Master Woke! Come inside for a pastry and meet Finn who has returned today after a visit to Sherborne."

John Woke reluctantly released the child, speaking something softly in his ear as he turned to join Alice and Finn. Ezekiel appeared at exactly the right moment and without further ado, they rode off, Ezekiel raising a hand towards Alice in farewell as they left.

Matthias was surprised to see that Alice had apparently invited John Woke to join her in the kitchen – he had decided to say some strong words of admonition to Finn, warning him also of the need to be neutral in any ensuing trouble. He had learned from Sir Tobias of increasing disturbances not only within Sherborne but also right along the South coast, the very worst being in Sussex and Kent. Although these shires were many miles distant, news travelled and young men, some young women too, were arming themselves for trouble. He did not think the unrest in those distant shires would influence peaceful Dorset but there was most undoubtably unease, conflict, resentment building locally. It seemed to be mostly towards Abbot Bradford and the often-absent Bishop Ayscough.

He raised an eyebrow discreetly at Alice, who nodded imperceptibly to him, so he sighed with resignation and eased his boots off before joining them with what appeared to be the obligatory pastry. John Woke finished his as Matthias took his first bite. Finn looked on in bemusement. When was he going to be told what his fate was – would he be asked to leave his studies? Was Master Barton going to accompany him home and tell his father not to send him again?

"Let's hear Finn's account of his day, please," Matthias said, brushing crumbs from his jerkin.

Finn told the story once more Alice noticing with interest how John Woke's normally deliberately bland expression changed. His colour rose, his breathing became more rapid, he kept his eyes on the ground, no longer looking at any of them. Matthias watched him carefully; it would seem he would have liked to sink out of sight, and as Finn completed his story, John Woke declared himself unwell and needed to retire to his chamber. Matthias detained him firmly.

"Are you the man wounded by Finn's half brothers? The story adds up perfectly – apart from the name given by the Jolifs – John of Mottisfont. Who are you? What interest do you have in the child Arnet?"

Finn was startled. He suddenly saw the truth of what Master Barton was suggesting. How could he have been so dense? But now he listened carefully, mouth slightly open in wonderment. He only saw Matthias as a schoolmaster – now he saw him as an informer to the Coroner, astute, aware of events, clear headed. Finn saw much to admire in his school master.

John Woke – or was he John of Mottisfont – tried to release himself from Matthias' grasp, but Matthias held firmly, blocking his exit and forcing him down onto a chair.

Alice heard the children's voices and detached herself from the group, meeting the girls and Lindy and directing them upstairs into the solar. She did not return.

"You are mistaken," began the man, recovering his composure somewhat. "I was simply talking to the group of waiting boys – I seek to teach, but it appears I am not trusted in this place."

"We need some honesty – Finn - where can we find your half brothers?"

"I honestly don't know where they live," Finn began, "but I did learn that the man they wounded had been brought to Milborne Port – I didn't add things up rightly. He is here, isn't he?"

John Woke rose as if in a trance.

"I am betrayed –" he whispered. "One little mistake is all I made."

There was a profound silence for a moment as Matthias took in what this must mean.

He suddenly forced John Woke's head down to run his fingers through his dark hair – and found what he expected.

"You have the strangest head of hair, John Woke. It appears there is a circle of thinner hair round your crown. How long ago did you leave your monastery?"

John Woke sank down in despair.

"All I needed was to make sure that my son is well cared for and happy," was his torn cry.

"John Woke – John of Mottisfont – what is your true name?"

"I am – I was – Brother Paul of Hyde Abbey, once of Sherborne Abbey. I am not sure who or what I am now. I have seen my son; he is a good lad – he is thriving. I am content. But what harm does that wicked harridan plan for him?"

Finn gasped, half understanding but not at all clear concerning his half-brothers' part in this turmoil. What a mess he seemed to have landed himself in – and he was bright enough to realise that Matthias would want him to remain silent about the revelation he had just heard. Finn knew this could not be the end yet.

Abbot Bradford had received the messenger from Hyde Abbey just as Brother Jonas was seeking an audience with Prior William. The Benedictine monks from Hyde were weary; Abbot Bradford ushered them into his sanctum, ordered refreshment for them and surveyed them with interest as they rested after their weary journey.

He was disturbed to learn of their mission however, when he felt they were rested sufficiently to explain their reason for such a journey.

Brother Paul. He who had caused the advent of the baby years ago, had disappeared from Hyde Abbey, where he had been sent as a safeguard against further involvement; The messengers did not know the reason for his transfer from Sherborne to Hyde - their message was simply from their abbot to ask whether Brother Paul had perchance returned to Sherborne for reasons of his own. Abbot Bradford had wasted no time; he sought the Coroner, told the story, heard Sir Tobias' suspicions that the man in Matthias' house was none other than this missing brother. Now Abbot Bradford felt he had the answer to the unpleasant whisperings in the Abbey concerning the parentage of the boy. It all seemed to be down to Brother Paul. As the Coroner left, Prior William came bustling in with yet more disturbing news.

"It seems, my lord Abbot, that Brother Jonas must seek a penance. He has confessed to me that he has been giving access to a brother of Hyde Abbey. He has been allowing him into the area of building to sleep for the last week at the least. He remembers him as Brother Paul – he who transferred to Hyde Abbey about six years ago – do you remember him?"

Indeed, Abbot Bradford had every cause to remember him.

"I am grieved to hear that one of our own brothers has become embroiled in this tale. The messengers from Hyde arrived just before you came to me – they were merely informing us that Brother Paul had disappeared and wanted to know whether he had come back here. By chance the Coroner was still in town; he had news of a stranger seeking work at his son in law's school. Between us we put two and two together. We should shortly be able to hear the whole sorry story – but first, I must needs tell you of the beginning of this tale of human failing and beg your forgiveness for believing I could carry this on my shoulders on behalf of us all."

Prior William was unaccustomed to hearing such humility from his Abbot, but bowed his head meekly as the two men went in search of Brother Jonas who would need to prostrate himself before his fellow monks as part of his penance.

Luke came across Artemesia keening once again, hugging herself with her thin arms, head bowed over her body as if in pain. She had been in the market place selling her healing herbs and fragrant flowers from the new stick refashioned after she had abandoned the tray Luke had made for her. Although there had been little love lost between the two women, so different in their lives, they had the bonds of sisterhood, nay, stronger than that for they had shared both a womb as well as their physical appearance. The bonds of twinship hold strong especially in death and when news of Dionisia's death reached her, Artemisia had abandoned her place in the market, ashamed to grieve for her sister in the rude gaze of crowds of people.

Luke sat on the ground beside her, waiting for the storm of grieving to lessen. He guessed she had no-one else to speak to, no-one else to care. He felt strangely responsible. He had wandered into the space in front of the Abbey in search of Merrick, his player friend who often sought the peace of the place. His lessons were completed for today and he had taken the opportunity to walk alone to exchange greetings with Merrick, if he were here. He had seen Artemisia rocking back and forth, huddled into herself, her heartfelt keening moving him to pause to give her comfort, young as he was.

He touched her hand softly, stroking it with his fingers. She roused a little, striving to see who sat beside her. Luke could sense the tension in her body, one of her hands was clasped tightly round something and as he continued to stroke the hand, she released her hold on the thing which tumbled unnoticed to the ground. Luke pushed it to one side the better to comfort her. After a little the keening ceased; she peered at Luke as one in a trance, her eyes unseeing, her body exhausted.

"Let me help you, Mistress," Luke offered. As before, Artemesia was unwilling to be escorted to her home, but she recognized the human kindness of the young scholar, the very same one who had helped her once before, when the pigs had destroyed her tray and who had taken the trouble to fashion a new tray for her.

"I thank you, young sir. My grief is for my sister, dead from burning this very day. She and I were not friends, but no-one deserves that pain, however much pain one has caused others. I must not be seen with you – our last meeting did not end well – an officer of the law threatened me with trouble for accepting your gift."

She stood up with difficulty, still dazed from shock and grief; Luke allowed her to leave, watching her stumble away as one blind, groping for her way, leaving her nosegays and stick behind – and the thing which had fallen from her hand unheeded. Luke picked it up curiously. He recognized the unmistakable form of Abbot Bradford, pins piercing the body in several places. As he regarded it, Luke suddenly felt rather sick. He was in no doubt of its purpose but he had not expected to find it with Artemisia, who he had come to regard as a gentle soul, sinned against rather than sinning. This smacked of witchcraft. He sought Thomas Copeland without further delay.

Abbot Bradford was testy towards his visitor who interrupted his interrogation of Brother Paul. Brother Jonas was waiting in the hall, head bowed in shame, Brother Francis beside him, detailed to ensure Brother Jonas stayed where he was told.

"Can it not wait, Master Copeland?"

"I don't believe so, my lord Abbot." So saying, Thomas Copeland placed the unpleasant but easily recognizable effigy on the table in front of the Abbot.

There was a stillness in the Abbot as he surveyed the likeness of himself, speared with sharp little pins.

"From where, might I ask, did you acquire this?" Abbot Bradford's tone was chilly.

Thomas explained succinctly.

"The woman must be arrested. My bailiff will deal with this now, Master Copeland."

Thomas felt himself dismissed, but before he finally closed the door, he felt it wise to let the Abbot know that the Coroner's grandson had seen the image – so no doubt the information would spread to the Coroner himself. In Thomas' view, this would be a fairer way of unravelling this odd story.

As the heavy door clicked closed, the Abbot turned to Brother Paul, listening from the shadows.

"Is this your work, Brother?"

Brother Paul was quick to deny all knowledge and the Abbot was inclined to believe him. The absence of a tonsure indicated that Brother Paul had been absent from his Abbey for some little while...and where was his habit? What was he thinking of to do such a thing? Brother Paul admitted that he had kept only his great cloak, now lost, as he had placed it over a wounded man in a field...another story to investigate...

For now, the Abbot sent reluctantly for Sir Tobias once more.

Artemisia was cleaning her few pots after a frugal meal when the bailiff found her. He was none too gentle, dismissing her protests and bundling her in front of him towards, eventually, the castle. She was shocked and terrified, unable to express her bewilderment at her apparent arrest.

As they passed the bottom of Cheap Street, Luke caught sight of her being prodded along roughly by the bailiff's men. He grabbed his cap and followed them, aware that he too might be in trouble for leaving without asking permission of Dame Maud. He dodged behind a thick hawthorn hedge to watch as the bailiff's men pushed Artemisia through a small postern and she was gone from his sight. Nonplussed about what to do next, Luke watched as another party approached the castle; he recognized Brother Francis for he had met him before, but walking beside him was a man whom Luke had seen before watching the school a short while back.

He hurried back to school fearful of being missed, and narrowly escaped meeting his grandfather leaving the Abbey to search for the Jolif boys.

CHAPTER TWELVE

The bond of twins

Artemisia found herself thrust rudely into a dirty cell; there were no rushes on the floor, the smell of human faeces and urine was strong; she crouched down near a damp wall and fearfully drew a faltering breath, trying to lift her skirts to cover her nose to deaden the odour. Her arms were bruised from the guards' rough hands as she had been hustled down the stone steps, pushed along by the bailiff's man, who wanted to be out of this hell hole as fast as possible.

She tried to think what she could possibly have done to warrant this arrest. She did not need a licence to sell her humble herbs, she had not stolen anything, there were no debts to others – she kept her life very simple to avoid the debt that had helped to kill her husband. She had recently given her sister a place to sleep, but she hadn't offered it – it had been demanded, and she had agreed, but Dionisia had only been with her for three or four nights before returning to her own hovel further down the hill. And now Dionisia was dead – burned to death in her own place. Could it be anything to do with the tray she had initially accepted from the scholar? She had not been soliciting favours or bribes – it was given as a simple gift. Oh, why was life so hard? Artemisia had picked her way carefully among the ashes of Dionisia's life, found nothing of any value, collected a bundle containing bits and pieces of shards, and suddenly overcome by the horror of burning to death, had clutched something from the bundle and thought to approach Allhallows church, beside the Abbey. Falling to her knees, she had been grieving for the life she and her sister had been born into, and the difference between them, but a twin was a twin and she felt bereft despite Dionisia's spiteful nature.

The jangle of the jailor's keys came nearer as Artemisia hugged herself to keep out the chill from the damp; the stout door was unlocked. The jailor pushed a man into the room, propping the door open with his booted foot.

"Is this the hag?" He growled at the man.

The stranger peered at Artemisia, her face now streaked with tears and dirt, her hair tangled.

"Yes. That's the hag who was with the two young men – she was wanting harm to come to Father Abbot."

The jailor aimed a kick at Artemisia before pushing the man out into the passage and slamming the door behind them both. Artemisia heard the key turn in the lock, the sound of their footsteps receding as they left.

Curse the identical nature of twins – she had been mistaken for her sister. With her sister now dead, who would believe her – worse, was the certain knowledge that even if her sister were still alive, she would still be here, for Dionisia would lie her way out of any trouble, sacrificing her twin sister to save her own skin. She sank down on the earth floor, all hope gone.

Luke was thoughtful and rather sad as the night approached. He felt he had read the old lady's character correctly and was dismayed that she was perhaps not what he thought. She had seemed such a gentle soul, sad but striving to make a slender living without recourse to begging. How could he have got it so wrong? Dame Maud was anxious for him; he seemed very withdrawn this evening, she felt. There were many such folk at this time, but Luke had felt touched by her simple herb bouquets, her refusal to give up. He wondered what she had done to be so treated by the bailiff and his men.

The Jolif boys kept themselves well hidden, out of town, out of sight. Daniel kept watch anxiously, aware that Noah's burns were serious, could fester, were causing him pain, discomfort, a degree of fever. They had managed to reach the common beyond the Northern edge of the town, the place from where they had released the pigs. Noah lay on the cool grass, moaning from time to time, face flushed with fever, burns beginning to fester. Daniel did not dare leave to find help until after dark, when he would visit the witch woman to obtain spells and potions to ease his brother. He knew they were now in serious trouble. Had anyone seen them leave Dionisia's house? Perhaps he would try and reach Finn, who surely now would help. But Finn had refused him only that morning. Maybe he could use the child at Milborne Port as a bargaining chip.....but that would mean leaving Noah on his own - Daniel remained watchful, his mind teeming with plans to extricate them from all blame for the fire and the death of Dionisia.

Matthias called on his friend Martin Cooper to request temporary help in the schoolroom. Martin was an old hand at this now, having helped Matthias in this way several times in the past, despite being crippled. The scholars loved Martin's visits, revering his bravery and enjoying the stories he could sometimes be persuaded to tell. He made certain that the disgraced monk - alias John Woke - alias John of Mottisfont – now Brother Paul, had not revealed details of his parentage to Arnet. Why should an innocent be burdened with the sins of his unknown father? He was relieved to find from Ezekiel that no such telling had happened.

He rode into Sherborne, joining Sir Tobias and his scribe at The George hostelry.

His father-in-law looked troubled, weary. He found the Abbot difficult to deal with; Abbot Bradford was a proud man who wished it to be known that Abbey affairs were his business, and had nothing to do with town affairs. Sir Tobias could not quite see eye to eye with him on this, particularly as this business appeared to be a twisted matter involving both Abbey and town. His scribe had prepared scrubbed tablets for notes and sat patiently waiting, sharpened quills ready. He watched Sir Tobias expectantly but so far, the Coroner had not uttered a word.

Matthias wondered whether his grasp of the recent events had escaped him, rendering the Coroner unable to put words down.

Sir Tobias sighed heavily, sinking down into the cushioned chair and passing his hand over his eyes.

"I'm afraid of the decline of law and order, Matthias. There is unrest spreading throughout the land, especially in the South and East – its tentacles are reaching even here. How do we stop the spread? How do we protect our young? What we have in front of us is a mere mischief – I am certain the Jolif brothers have stirred up trouble to amuse themselves but now we have an elderly woman incarcerated in the castle – how would such a woman allow herself to be involved with such as the Jolifs? Why did she have an effigy of the Abbot, stuck all over with wicked pins – witchcraft to frighten – what hold did she have over the Abbot? The Abbot has declined to allow me to speak with her. He tells me it was she who was spreading rumours and lies about Arnet's parentage and she will surely suffer for it."

Matthias listened to the rising despair in Sir Tobias' voice.

"When I attended the coronation of the queen in London I had such hopes. We should have an heir by now – his Grace the King should be firmly at the helm, steering his ship of destiny. Instead, he is farming, dreaming, promoting schools – yes, I know that will ultimately reap benefits, - but he must be more than a dreamer and a philosopher or philanthropist. The task of the king is to beget an heir and to lead his men into battle. His Grace has done neither. His nobles grapple for power and land. We are losing the war in France – our hold on lands won so dearly by the King's father are slipping away month by month, battle by battle, decision by decision. The commons from all shires are rising up in protest. It will spread to here, Matthias, and I don't know how I can prevent it."

Matthias raised a warning hand towards the scribe, open mouthed at his master's words.

"You will forget this conversation," he commanded him. "Sir Tobias spoke his heart without fear, and I would not have it repeated. You have not heard these sentiments."

The scribe, an old and trusted member of the family, nodded his head wisely.

Sir Tobias came to himself. He shook his head as if to clear a nightmare.

"Thank you Matthias. I must deal with the present, not fear for the future. Forgive me. I am still the King's man, body and soul."

"And I," responded Matthias, and a muttered agreement echoed from the scribe.

"So – what have we? I see we must now return to the very beginning."

"And what is the very beginning? The marriage of His Grace? Or the commencement of the unrest here in Sherborne?"

"One follows the other, Matthias. If we look to Sherborne, the beginning is surely the unrest and discontent between the Abbot and the citizens. We can go back as far as the terrible day when the font was smashed – and then the fire consuming much of the Abbey. Since then nothing has been resolved; the font has not been replaced, the narrow opening between Allhallows and the Abbey has not been attended to and the Abbot has squeezed the good people of Sherborne dry to pay for the repairs to the Abbey. In exchange, they have started to plague him with little disturbances, outright offences and not so subtle damages. On the credit side, the alms-houses have been completed, which unfortunately increased the Abbot's indignation. Folk worked hard and gave willingly to raise the money for the building. His Grace licenced it, the alms-houses are now complete – but the Abbey remains in scaffolding."

The list lengthened, the scratch of the quill speeding up as Sir Tobias listed the sequence of events going back more than six years.

"It is further complicated now," Matthias commented, "with the realisation that there is much discontent in our Southern and Western shires, spreading daily with young men unafraid to kick against the traces. We see it even here, but your Jolif boys – they don't have the same aim as the real trouble makers. They would be a thorn in anyone's side anywhere at any time. They don't seem to have the aims of the silent protesters."

"One thing is becoming clear to me, Matthias; plainly the Jolifs are a domestic issue; the men, and even some women, who are causing deliberate damage to property owned by the Bishop and the Abbot are a different breed. When the unrest reaches here, as it undoubtably will, they will be the ones who will join with other factions further up country and agitate against the failing state of our country."

Matthias noted that the Coroner did not mention his Grace the king again, but the implication was there.

"I will find those brothers and make them stand trial; they are a scourge on our town. The other faction – they have caused no hurt or damage to persons, except the blow to Edmund – and they have formed a protective barrier around that incident. However, we may well have a lead from the cloak which this pesky monk placed over the injured man. I would speak with him, whether the Abbot says yes or no."

"I understand the castle reported a small break in recently – is this more of the protesters, showing their increasing anger at their high rents, taxes, croukpenny on their ale -or was it your beleaguered monk?"

"Very little damage was done – some papers scattered, inks spilled, and all in the rooms of my lord Bishop. I suspect it was done with the help of someone working in the castle – and as so little fuss has been made, it appears that there is much support for these disturbances. My guess is that whoever led that incident simply wanted it known that entry to the castle was not a huge difficulty. However, security was tightened after the event."

"The fish pond draining?"

The ghost of a smile crossed the Coroner's lips.

"The Abbot has paid his fine for allowing the flood to impinge on highways. Whether his bailiff has found the culprits, I have no idea."

Matthias pondered on the sequence of events.

"We have left the child Arnet out of all this," he said slowly, wondering which of these troublesome groups was responsible for Arnet's admission to his school.

"Ah. Yes. This is another branch of our ever-growing plot to consider. I think it is time to force ourselves on Abbot Bradford."

Ezekiel was known by many of the marketeers and their clientele who often sought him out for advice; this was how he had first come to know Matthias. In town now, he dug out a painful splinter from a stonemason's hand, dressing it carefully when the pus and poison had finished oozing; he gave a salve to the bakehouse boy from one ale house – the burn looked semi-healed, but the lad was a whiner and needed comfort. He chatted with other stall holders leaving his bag open in case there were any others needing him. As he turned away to speak with another, the bakehouse boy shouted suddenly, "Stop thief! Mister! He's pinched some salves!"

Ezekiel turned swiftly and gave chase to the young man who had darted away through the crowds. The cry of thief followed him and he was brought to the ground by a burly fletcher.

"For shame!" Mistress Saddler proclaimed, "If you needed salves, Master Jacobson sometimes gives them freely. What are you thinking - get on your feet."

The leather worker's wife was a well-built woman with strong muscles, and she grasped Daniel firmly and hauled him up. The fletcher leered unpleasantly at him as he marched him back to Ezekiel, who by now had returned to his booth where the market reeve was waiting for the thief. The reeve was delighted by their catch.

"I did hear that the Coroner was looking for you and your brother. I've spotted the Coroner in town this morning. That's a nice surprise for him. Where's your brother?"

Daniel wriggled and shuffled but did not answer. He glared round, eyes darting to the left and right seeking an escape route, but the fletcher was a match for him, holding him tightly.

"Pesky pair, these two," declared the fletcher, happy to hand Daniel over to the reeve.

Ezekiel began to close his bag, packing his ointments carefully away. He would need to accompany the reeve to accuse Daniel of theft.

"Why did you need to steal?" he asked the young man.

"It's nothing to you," came the sulky answer, but Daniel's eyes were wary, and Ezekiel guessed the sulk was a front for fear.

They found the Coroner easily, just leaving the George Inn, Matthias and the scribe with him. Ezekiel was not surprised to see Matthias, - his absence from the schoolroom had warned him something was happening.

"Well, talk of the Devil!" The Coroner exclaimed, as he saw Daniel. "Where's that fine brother of yours?"

Daniel scowled. He remained silent.

"Time to see the Abbot. We'll take this Jolif boy with us. Do you want to charge him with theft as well as murder, Master Jacobson?"

"Murder?" the shriek came from Daniel, startled from his silence.

"Yes, murder, general disturbance and now thieving. Where's your brother?"

Daniel gave in. Noah was in a bad way; he needed help and for once in his rotten life he was afraid.

"In a corner of Saddler's field. He's really bad."

Ezekiel and the reeve were on their way to Saddler's field to bring him in.

The Abbot received the party with his usual arrogant reluctance. However, the Coroner was abrupt with him when he declared that Brother Paul's misdeeds were purely Abbey business.

"My lord Abbot. Let's not beat about the bush any further. You recently came to me with a problem concerning your good name within the Abbey. I have spent some time investigating this, together with Master Barton, who has put himself at considerable inconvenience. This is the business of all here, and it is possible that this thieving young man accosted in the market place just now for stealing may be able to shed a little light on the death of the woman found burnt to death."

Matthias noted that Daniel paled at the words. It seemed Daniel was unaware that she had died.

Abbot Bradford was grateful for the lack of detail about his problem within the Abbey, given the presence of Master Jacobson and Daniel Jolif. He softened his attitude accordingly.

"I will summon Brother Paul. I can tell you that he is guilty of nothing more than leaving Hyde Abbey – absconding – breaking his vows – he is returning to Hyde Abbey tomorrow where the Abbot there will decide his fate."

Brother Paul came silently in, accompanied by Prior William. He looked shamefaced when he saw Matthias, reached out to him, but Matthias turned away. He was not ready to accept an apology until he had heard the story.

"We must deal first with this young man," Sir Tobias said, indicating Daniel.

"This is one of the men who accosted me. Took me to see the hag I saw in the castle yesterday –"

Daniel listened to this with a ray of hope – Dionisia was still alive. This man had identified her!

"I would have nothing to do with her search for information about the child – I could not understand why she needed to know details of his parentage -I walked away from the unclean place – a miasma of mischief brewing, only to have a knife in my back."

Abbot Bradford raised his eyes incredulously to Brother Paul.

"**SHE** wanted to know about the child?" he expostulated, glaring with indignation at Daniel.

Daniel tightened his lips, refusing to add another word. If he said nothing they would not be able to charge him with wounding - -after all, it was his brother who had thrown the knife. Matthias read his mind and grasped his arm, twisting it behind his back, forcing him to his knees.

"You have tried to corrupt your half brother Finn, dragging him into your filthy lies; You sought him out at my home; you WILL answer questions put to you or I will see both you and your brother hang for perpetual attempts on innocent lives." Matthias' anger at the dumb insolence of this man made him scarcely articulate – spitting his wrath out.

The Coroner held up his hand to calm Matthias.

"These men are known to me, Matthias. I appreciate your hot words but have no fear – I aim to deal harshly – justly – but harshly with my fine friend here."

"This is a tale much tangled," the Abbot sighed, as Ezekiel Jacobson, the port reeve and between them shuddering, shivering and clearly in pain, Noah staggered in to the gathering.

Abbot Bradford sent a messenger for men to take Daniel to the castle, while Brother Francis appeared to help Noah to a pallet in the infirmary, guarded by two monks. Ezekiel and the reeve accompanied them. Daniel was much subdued by the state of his brother, now unable to speak coherently, ugly burns disfiguring his face, angry, red and suppurating. He was unable to bear any pressure on his hands, burned raw on the palms and Brother Francis and Ezekiel were forced to support him as best they could without causing him further pain.

"These were the two men whom I observed in the fields with sheep, Father Abbot, when I was sleeping in the open. Then I became aware that there were two groups – but it was not these two who caused the bailiff's death." Brother Paul began, when their conclave had settled into a more discreet gathering.

"The bailiff recovered, Brother Paul," observed Sir Tobias. "Probably helped by the mysterious cloak thrown over him. That was yours, was it not?"

Brother Paul admitted that it was. He explained that he could not refuse to help the man, who had been doing what he saw as his duty – and that party of men were more sober, older than the two brothers and their raucous friends.

"You know now that I am the father of the child Arnet. I have compounded my initial sin by leaving the Abbey which has given me support for the last six years. I have become unnaturally obsessed with needing to know that my son is well cared for. I simply wanted to see him, assure myself that he is loved. I was desperate to touch him, look into his eyes to make sure I had not done him such a great injustice as to be born fatherless and unwanted. I was unaware of this woman's interest in my son – " Abbot Bradford held up his hand in warning.

"It cannot be, Brother Paul. You must refer to him by name only, - or simply as the child."

Brother Paul bowed his head in submission; Matthias was shaken by the pain in the monk's eyes.

"The child was of interest to the woman – I still do not understand why. She wanted to know the true parentage of the child – she had an effigy in her hand of Father Abbot. It smacked of evil – it was riven with pins. I left, but one of the brothers we have just encountered was angry because I would not give them information."

Sir Tobias was thoughtful. "It seems to me, my lord Abbot, that we need to see this woman. I suggest the rumours of parentage have emanated from her. If that is so, she has done great harm, for although the two brothers are the cause of some trouble in the town, it is not the same irritations which caused the flood from your fish ponds, nor the repeated sheep troubles. The brothers are the sons of a previous outlaw – they have known nothing but mischief and disobedience all their lives. I have no doubt that they were the force behind the pig incident – that is their sort of trouble."

Matthias volunteered to visit Mistress Amice to prepare her for the welcome homecoming of her son, Arnet. There would be no need for her to know any more of the tangled details.

CHAPTER THIRTEEN

Matthias' shame

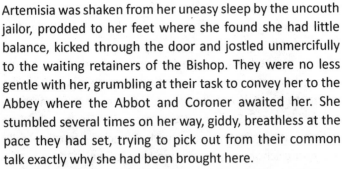

Artemisia was shaken from her uneasy sleep by the uncouth jailor, prodded to her feet where she found she had little balance, kicked through the door and jostled unmercifully to the waiting retainers of the Bishop. They were no less gentle with her, grumbling at their task to convey her to the Abbey where the Abbot and Coroner awaited her. She stumbled several times on her way, giddy, breathless at the pace they had set, trying to pick out from their common talk exactly why she had been brought here.

She was overawed by the splendour of the Coroner as she saw him, although he was no more splendid than was normal; it was his chain of office which frightened and awed her, and she fought to keep back the tears. Abbot Bradford towered over her, his black robes giving him the look of a marauding crow and his eyes glittered with purpose as he folded his arms, tucking his hands inside his robe. He breathed deeply and noisily as he surveyed her. She felt her legs buckling, and it was Matthias who caught her as she fell, tucking a crude stool under her to prevent her from collapsing completely. In her distress she did not recognize him as the man who had spoken so roughly to her when Luke had offered her the newly made herb tray.

The three men surveyed her in silence. The Coroner had long ago learned the value of silence to force speech from those accused whilst the Abbot was for once bereft of words as he observed the pitiful figure before him. Matthias absorbed the bruises, scrapes and bloodied fingernails; his brain told him that something was amiss here, but he looked to Sir Tobias for guidance.

"You have been accused of spreading malicious and deceitful untruths about my lord Abbot, interfering with a domestic household in our town, and far worse – indulging in practices relating to witch-craft."

Artemisia looked up from the stool which Matthias had placed for her.

She opened her mouth to speak but no words would come; her tears fell on her withered hands; how had she come to this? What help could she expect from these powerful men? She knew this man; it was he who had warned her against speaking with the child – hardly a child – a young scholar who had been kind to her.

The Abbot placed the effigy of himself beset with pins on the table in front of her.

"You are indulging in witchcraft. This is punishable by death. What have you to say?"

"This is all I have left of my sister," she whispered, broken and terrified.

"You are lying," the Abbot uttered, harshly. He would see this harridan beaten into submission and confession.

"Where did you obtain this article from, my lord Abbot?" The Coroner's question was more of a comment for interest than pertinent to the case.

"Master Copeland brought it to me. A scholar of his found it on the woman. It is proof of her guilt."

"A scholar? What was a scholar doing entangled in this business?" Matthias had Finn in mind, but how would Finn have had connection to Master Copeland.

"You have involved young minds in your filthy witchcraft habits," Abbot Bradford declared. His eyes were shining with zeal as he felt he was closing the case against this specimen, huddled in front of him.

"Might we have conversation with Master Copeland? I am concerned for the scholar who may not realise the wickedness of witchcraft." Matthew remembered Finn's unexplained day of absenteeism.

Master Copeland was summoned.

"Of course I remember the scholar who had this item," he said, "it was your grandson, Sir Tobias."

Matthias felt his bowels turn to water, his blood to ice. This was a stunning blow. How could this have happened? He felt physically sick. What had induced him to touch such a thing? When had he, Matthias, not noticed signs of disaffection with normality? He felt the Coroner's hand on his arm.

"There must be an explanation for this, Matthias. Stay calm. Luke must tell us himself what his purpose is."

Thomas Copeland departed to fetch Luke. Matthew waited, his mind teeming with guilt at not noticing signs in his son, of fury towards the woman crouched on the stool, head bowed, arms tightly round her skinny frame. Matthias noticed she was shivering uncontrollably.

Abbot Bradford was impatient. As far as he was concerned, the matter was nearing its end. She would be made to suffer the punishment for witchcraft and he would be able to put these rumours and lies behind him. The recalcitrant monk Brother Paul would not be his business; the rumours would recede. All would be well.

Luke was surprised at being summoned to the Abbey. Thomas Copeland warned him that his grandfather and his step father were present and that it would be wise if he were to be polite. Luke felt a little offended by this; he had no inclination to be anything but polite, - he knew his manners.

They entered the Abbot's cool, well ordered sanctum silently, Luke overawed by the sight of the Coroner in working mode. Luke had only ever seen his grandfather as family, warm, loving, generous. He looked at his working face now and was stunned by the difference. The Coroner was every inch the upright justice, stern of face, eagle of eye, unsmiling as he surveyed the piteous form of Amelisia, crouched on the stool.

The Abbot was smirking with success; the culprit was caught; soon the strange story would unravel and he could punish this crone who had spread such slander and spite against him, undermining the very core of his control.

Matthias stared at Luke, striving to uphold him to be truthful and honest. If Luke had become involved in any way with this dreadful woman, he would do his very best to undo the harm done to Luke's young mind with love and understanding.

Now he bent to the woman, his face on her level.

"Mistress," he said gently, "look at this scholar. Do you know him?"

She looked up fearfully, first at Matthias, then beyond him to where the boy was standing aghast at the solemn scene, her tears still coursing unchecked down her seamed face.

"I do know him, sir," she whispered, "He helped me to stand when I fell on the Abbey green after the pigs ran down the hill."

"What difference does that make to her guilt?" Abbot Bradford grated harshly, the smile disappearing from his face.

Luke crouched down beside Amelisia. She squinted at him through her unchecked tears.

"Mistress, how did you come to be in this trouble?"

"The question should be, Luke, how did you come to be involved in this matter?" Matthias sounded cold, despite the break in his voice.

Luke stood tall in front of the imposing figure of Abbot Bradford and his grandfather. He looked beyond them to the stranger who he had seen once or twice watching the school, although now he came to think of it, not since Arnet had moved out. He saw the tremble in the lower lip of his step father who was pale, looking coldly at Amelisia, still shivering on the stool.

"Amelisia is the herb seller for whom I made the wooden tray," Luke was speaking directly and urgently to Matthias. "She has a pitch at the bottom of Cheap Street. The pigs knocked her over. I made a tray for her, but it is broken again now. Someone told her she could not accept a gift. Then I found her again, grieving after her sister had died in the fire. This was the only thing of her sister's that she could find after the fire."

Amelisia raised her head and looked at Luke.

"It was the only thing left of my twin. We were not friends – she was always trouble but a twin is special. There is always a blood bond and it is now broken. Half of me has disappeared. I am no longer whole."

Luke could think of nothing to say to this; he stood awkwardly, facing Abbot Bradford. He had only ever seen the Abbot from a distance, and he was overawed as he realised he had made no respectful bow to this haughty presence, still filling the room with his righteous indignation.

The man who was a stranger spoke, meekly.

"Father Abbot, I do not believe this is the same woman who threatened me. She is physically identical, indeed her twin, but there is no air of malevolence. You are speaking to the wrong person."

Silence filled the room. Matthias was filled with sweet relief, fighting against his instinct to sweep Luke into a hug, but there were matters to lay to rest, including his own hot rush of shame as he recalled how harshly he had spoken to her.

"With Dionisia gone, we can only use the Jolif brothers' testimony for evidence. It appears that she thought she had some idea of the boy Arnet's parentage, quite wrongly and sought to gain through blackmail with information. She had come before me many times for listening to neighbour's affairs, sneaking around, causing troubles between husbands and wives. I did not think she would aim so high."

Abbot Bradford shot the Coroner a warning glance.

"My lord Abbot, I will now question the Jolif brothers who will face more serious charges."

Luke knelt to Amelisia. He touched her gently on her knee.

"Mistress, I think you are free to go?" He looked questioningly towards Matthias and Sir Tobias.

"Yes, indeed," Sir Tobias agreed. He picked a cloak from behind the Abbot's door and placed it round her shivering form.

"I'm sure the good Abbot will give you his spare cloak in recompense for your wrongful arrest."

Without another word to the open-mouthed Abbot, Sir Tobias stalked out to find the Jolifs.

"Where did you find the name John of Mottisfont?" Matthias asked, painfully aware that he should make amends to Amelisia, mistaking her for Dionisia.

"It is not a Benedictine abbey, so I hoped it would deflect from my purpose and give me extra cover. I am to return to Hyde tomorrow to face whatever the Abbot shall decide. I allowed my obsession to override my vows. It will be whatever the Abbot decrees. However, I have seen what I came to see and I shall return to whatever punishment with good will. Allow me to apologise to you and your gracious wife for the deceit, and to thank you for the hospitality of your home."

Matthias bowed to him in acknowledgment, but he knew he had some apologies of his own to make.

"Allow me to apologise for my rough words to you, mistress. I had just been shown your sister...I honestly thought you were one and the same person. My son has dealt with you more kindly than I have."

Luke looked at his father askance.

"Amelisia is gentle and knows much about herbs, Father. Mistress, let me help you home."

Amelisia allowed Luke to raise her from the stool. He adjusted the Abbot's cloak round her shoulders and fastened the fine jewelled clasp. Matthias watched him, then together they escorted the woman from the room.

Sir Tobias made haste to the castle, where he demanded to see Daniel Jolif.

Daniel was much chastened, not surprisingly. He and his brother had always acted together, and as Amelisia told them, one without the other is not a whole person. The bond of twins, once broken, has a strong influence on life's path.

Despite that, there was much bluster, bragging and pretended indifference to their fate. Daniel eventually reached the nub of the saga – how Dionisia felt she knew enough about the parentage of the child Arnet to ascribe him to the Abbot. He did have the grace to admit that he and his brother thought this unlikely and highly amusing, but Dionysia became obsessed by the idea of making the Abbot pay for her silence. He described how he and Noah had traced Arnet to Milborne Port where they found their half brother Finn, who refused to help them. The story became more sombre from thence. Sir Tobias had his own methods for forcing a confession from Daniel regarding the wounding of John of Mottisfont, the knifing of Dionisia, but Daniel resolutely refused to admit to the deliberate act of ensuring that the woman burnt to death. He would only say that some ash and sparks had been tossed around and he thought she would scramble out of the way.

When Sir Tobias remarked that she had been wounded as well, he was evasive.

As the Coroner walked back to the Abbey to interview Noah Jolif he pondered the sad fate which must await the pair. They had caused much public nuisance, used knives against citizens – he could not really describe either of the victims as honest citizens, but citizens had a right to their personal safety against such reckless men. They had undoubtedly caused the death of Dionisia, whichever one of them had acted he would probably never know, and they had attempted to corrupt young Finn. He could see no reason to recommend anything other than hanging.

Brother Francis was not hopeful of the outcome for Noah. His burns had festered through initial neglect and infection. His face was disfigured, the burns to his face had come perilously close to his eyes which were bandaged now. He was not conscious enough for the Coroner to have any meaningful answers from him, and Sir Tobias left with a heavy heart. Hanging always caused him unease and an unsettled feeling.

Ezekiel was leaving the Abbey at the same time as the Coroner. He had given Brother Francis all the help he could with Noah, and now he would return home. He felt it was only a matter of time for Noah; maybe if Daniel had explained and sought help for Noah sooner the outcome might have been different, although that chance was slim – Noah had fallen onto flames and his burns were deeply severe.

Matthias had taken Luke back to Thomas Copeland and now the three men met before returning home. They would ride a little way together before dividing towards their own homes.

"The Abbot is satisfied now. The rumours will die away, Brother Jonas will do penance, Brother Paul will return to face the Abbot of Hyde and Brother Francis will tend to Noah until the end. He will not live, I fear."

Matthias was restless as he listened to Sir Tobias.

"Luke and I walked Mistress Amelisia to her home. She has some knowledge of herbs and flora. I would like to sponsor a small market stall for her. It could be of use to you, Ezekiel. She is a gentle soul who strives to be independent. I wronged her and I would like to help her rebuild. Can you arrange it for me?

Sir Tobias agreed that it would be possible. The sponsorship would involve the payment of market tax and the provision of a suitable stall, which Matthias was pleased to be able to do. Ezekiel joined the gesture by agreeing to provide some simple tinctures for her to sell.

"The problem of civil unrest is not solved," Sir Tobias sighed, his mind still lingering on the Abbey versus the town.

"I doubt it will be with such tales of disobedience and riots coming to us via travellers. There is something coming towards us which I do not like to think about. Too much rests with His Grace, and he is not taking control of his lords and barons. Here in Sherborne, we should lie low."

All three men agreed soberly as they each went their own ways.

Finn made his own way into Sherborne some time later. He had a satisfactory interview with Master Barton – well, as satisfactory as it could be. He understood that whatever he had learned was confidential; he had no difficulty with that. He was gently chastised for skipping school and there had followed advice relative to his loyalties towards his grace the King. Finn was sceptical about that. He was developing his own ideas, and had come into Sherborne specifically to make contact with the men described by his father as the young hotheads. Finn wanted to be one of them, and was prepared to seek until he found them. The mischief his half brothers had involved themselves in was none of his business and certainly held no interest from his father, the miller, who made it clear that they were nothing to do with him. Finn was acutely aware of social injustices and understood more of the poor leadership than a lad of his age should.

It was a heady mix, holding a forewarning of tragic events to come.

Author's notes.

As far as possible, I have followed the beginning of the reign of Henry VI - he was a poor king, indecisive although philanthropic towards education and architecture. His queen Margaret was happy with him to start with, but as time went on, this soured. More of that in the next, final book.

The nobility was certainly gearing up for civil war – Lancastrians versus Yorkists – and the emergence of the character of Finn shows how the young may have decided to throw their loyalty behind Richard of York.

Bishop Ayscough is a real character. He was the confessor to Henry VI, as well as being the bishop of Salisbury, and when in the area his home was Sherborne Castle. Abbot Bradford is also a real character, always at odds with the people of Sherborne because of the fire and the battle of the fonts. He did not, however, have anything to do with a baby. That is my imagination and serves to highlight his unbending character, pride and haughty nature.

There was unrest in the town – it stemmed from the high rents, taxes and general unrest. There were men – and probably some women – who caused deliberate acts of civil disobedience to irritate the situation. Those not involved in these acts often refused to betray their neighbours, forming a wall of silence round them. This will be particularly true in the next, final book in this series.

I'm sorry there is no actual murder in this book! I didn't want Sherborne and Milborne Port to become like Midsummer murders.....that must be the worst possible village for murders!

Dionisia was a real person, stirring up discord amongst her neighbours and was genuinely before the law on several occasions, however, there is much about her that is pure invention. The inclusion of two sets of twins is my own take on the story. As the mother of twins myself I know something of the bond felt by twins, especially when it is broken.

The families mentioned were genuine Sherborne people – Coker...Hoddinotte...Fletcher...Goffe, and the father of the Jolif twins was a real outlaw who was hanged some time before this story begins. Sherborne has such a rich vein of material for writing – it is hard to resist.

The sixth book will reveal the political leanings of my main characters as the Cousin's War begins...otherwise known as the Wars of the Roses. It will jump several years and will show how every day people came to choose to support one side or the other...with tragic results.